The Means of Escape

Also by Penelope Fitzgerald

The Means of Escape

STORIES

PENELOPE FITZGERALD

Flamingo
An Imprint of HarperCollins*Publishers*

Flamingo
An Imprint of HarperCollins*Publishers*
77–85 Fulham Palace Road,
Hammersmith, London W6 8JB

www.**fire**and**water**.com

Flamingo is a registered trade mark of
HarperCollins*Publishers* Limited

First published in Great Britain by Flamingo 2000

1 3 5 7 9 8 6 4 2

A catalogue record for this book
is available from the British Library

These stories are works of fiction. The names,
characters and incidents portrayed in them are the work of the
author's imagination. Any resemblance to actual persons, living
or dead, events or localities, is entirely coincidental.

ISBN 0 00 710030 2

Set in Postscript Linotype Spectrum with Janson display by
Rowland Phototypesetting Ltd, Bury St Edmunds, Suffolk

Printed and bound in Great Britain by
Omnia Books Limited, Glasgow

CONTENTS

The Means of Escape

The Means of Escape

St George's Church, Hobart, stands high above Battery Point and the harbour. Inside, it looks strange and must always have done so, although (at the time I'm speaking of) it didn't have the blue, pink and yellow-patterned stained glass that you see there now. That was ordered from a German firm in 1875. But St George's has always had the sarcophagus-shaped windows which the architect had thought Egyptian and therefore appropriate (St George is said to have been an Egyptian saint). They give you the curious impression, as you cross the threshold, of entering a tomb.

In 1852, before the organ was installed, the church used to face east, and music was provided by a seraphine. The seraphine was built, and indeed invented, by a Mr Ellard, formerly of Dublin, now a resident of Hobart. He intended it to suggest the angelic choir, although the singing voices at his disposal – the surveyor general, the naval chaplain, the harbourmaster and their staffs – were for the most part male. Who was able to play the seraphine? Only, at first, Mr Ellard's daughter, Mrs Logan, who seems to have got £20 a year for doing so, the same fee as the clerk and the sexton. When Mrs Logan began to feel the task was too much for her – the seraphine needs continuous pumping – she instructed Alice Godley, the Rector's daughter.

Hobart stands 'south of no north', between snowy Mount Wellington and the River Derwent, running down over steps and promontories to the harbour's bitterly cold water. You get all the winds that blow. The next stop to the south is the limit of the Antarctic drift ice. When Alice came up to practise the hymns she had to unlock the outer storm door, made of Huon pine, and the inner door, also a storm door, and drag them shut again.

The seraphine stood on its own square of Axminster carpet in the transept. Outside (at the time I'm speaking of) it was a bright afternoon, but inside St George's there was that mixture of light and inky darkness which suggests that from the darkness something may be about to move. It was difficult, for instance, to distinguish whether among the black-painted pews, at some distance away, there was or wasn't some person or object rising above the level of the seats. Alice liked to read mystery stories, when she could get hold of them, and the thought struck her now, 'The form of a man is advancing from the shadows.'

If it had been ten years ago, when she was still a school-girl, she might have shrieked out, because at that time there were said to be bolters and escaped convicts from

Port Arthur on the loose everywhere. The Constabulary hadn't been put on to them. Now there were only a few names of runaways, perhaps twenty, posted up on the notice boards outside Government House.

'I did not know that anyone was in the church,' she said. 'It is kept locked. I am the organist. Perhaps I can assist you?'

A rancid stench, not likely from someone who wanted to be shown round the church, came towards her up the aisle. The shape, too, seemed wrong. But that, she saw, was because the head was hidden in some kind of sack like a butchered animal, or, since it had eyeholes, more like a man about to be hung.

'Yes,' he said, 'you can be of assistance to me.'

'I think now that I can't be,' she said, picking up her music case. 'No nearer,' she added distinctly.

He stood still, but said, 'We shall have to get to know one another better.' And then, 'I am an educated man. You may try me out if you like, in Latin and some Greek. I have come from Port Arthur. I was a poisoner.'

'I should not have thought you were old enough to be married.'

'I never said I poisoned my wife!' he cried.

'Were you innocent, then?'

'You women think that everyone in gaol is innocent. No, I'm not innocent, but I was wrongly incriminated. I never lifted a hand. They criminated me on false witness.'

'I don't know about lifting a hand,' she said. 'You mentioned that you were a poisoner.'

'My aim in saying that was to frighten you,' he said. 'But that is no longer my aim at the moment.'

It had been her intention to walk straight out of the church, managing the doors as quickly as she could, and on no account looking back at him, since she believed that with a man of bad character, as with a horse, the best thing was to show no emotion whatever. He, however, moved round through the pews in such a manner as to block her way.

He told her that the name he went by, which was not his given name, was Savage. He had escaped from the Model Penitentiary. He had a knife with him, and had thought at first to cut her throat, but had seen almost at once that the young lady was not on the cross. He had got into the church tower (which was half finished, but no assigned labour could be found to work on it at the moment) through the gaps left in the brickwork. Before he could ask for food she told him firmly that she herself could get him none. Her father was the incumbent, and the most generous of men, but at the Rectory they had to keep very careful count of everything, because charity was given out at the door every Tuesday and Thursday evening. She might be able to bring him the spent tea-leaves, which were always kept, and he could mash them again if he could find warm water.

'That's a sweet touch!' he said. 'Spent tea-leaves!'

'It is all I can do now, but I have a friend — I may perhaps be able to do more later. However, you can't stay here beyond tomorrow.'

'I don't know what day it is now.'

'It is Wednesday, the twelfth of November.'

'Then *Constancy* is still in harbour.'

'How do you know that?'

It was all they did know, for certain, in the penitentiary. There was a rule of absolute silence, but the sailing lists were passed secretly between those who could read, and memorized from them by those who could not.

'*Constancy* is a converted collier, carrying cargo and a hundred and fifty passengers, laying at Franklin Wharf. I am entrusting you with my secret intention, which is to stow on her to Portsmouth, or as far at least as Cape Town.'

He was wearing grey felon's slops. At this point he took off his hood, and stood wringing it round and round in his hands, as though he was trying to wash it.

Alice looked at him directly for the first time.

'I shall need a change of clothing, ma'am.'

'You may call me "Miss Alice",' she said.

At the prompting of some sound, or imaginary sound, he retreated and vanished up the dark gap, partly boarded up, of the staircase to the tower. That which had been on his head was left in a heap on the pew. Alice took it up and put it into her music case, pulling the strap tight.

She was lucky in having a friend very much to her own mind, Aggie, the daughter of the people who ran Shuckburgh's Hotel; Aggie Shuckburgh, in fact.

'He might have cut your throat, did you think of that?'

'He thought better of it,' said Alice.

'What I should like to know is this: why didn't you go straight to your father, or to Colonel Johnson at the Constabulary? I don't wish you to answer me at once, because it mightn't be the truth. But tell me this: would you have acted in the same manner, if it had been a woman hiding in the church?' Alice was silent, and Aggie said, 'Did a sudden strong warmth spring up between the two of you?'

'I think that it did.'

No help for it, then, Aggie thought. 'He'll be hard put to it, I'm afraid. There's no water in the tower, unless the last lot of builders left a pailful, and there's certainly no dunny.' But Alice thought he might slip out by night. 'That is what I should do myself, in his place.' She explained that Savage was an intelligent man, and that he intended to stow away on *Constancy*.

'My dear, you're not thinking of following him?'

'I'm not thinking at all,' said Alice.

They were in the hotel, checking the clean linen. So many tablecloths, so many aprons, kitchen, so many aprons, dining-room, so many pillow shams. They hardly ever talked without working. They knew their duties to both their families.

Shuckburgh's had its own warehouse and bond store on the harbour front. Aggie would find an opportunity to draw out, not any of the imported goods, but at least a ration of tea and bacon. Then they could see about getting it up to the church.

'As long as you didn't imagine it, Alice!'

Alice took her arm. 'Forty-five!'

They had settled on the age of forty-five to go irredeemably cranky. They might start imagining anything they liked then. The whole parish, indeed the whole neighbourhood, thought that they were cranky already, in any case, not to get settled, Aggie in particular, with all the opportunities that came her way in the hotel trade.

'He left this behind,' said Alice, opening her music case, which let fly a feral odour. She pulled out the sacking mask, with its slits, like a mourning pierrot's, for eyes.

'Do they make them wear those?'

'I've heard Father speak about them often. They wear them every time they go out of their cells. They're part of the new system, they have to prove their worth. With the masks on, none of the other prisoners can tell who a man is, and he can't tell who they are. He mustn't speak either, and that drives a man into himself, so that he's alone with the Lord, and can't help but think over his wrongdoing and repent. I never saw one of them before today, though.'

'It's got a number on it,' said Aggie, not going so far as to touch it. 'I dare say they put them to do their own laundry.'

*　　*　　*

At the Rectory there were five people sitting down already to the four o'clock dinner. Next to her father was a guest, the visiting preacher; next to him was Mrs Watson, the housekeeper. She had come to Van Diemen's Land with a seven-year sentence, and now had her ticket to leave. Assigned servants usually ate in the backhouse, but in the Rector's household all were part of the same family. Then, the Lukes. They were penniless immigrants (his papers had Mr Luke down as a scene-painter, but there was no theatre in Hobart). He had been staying, with his wife, for a considerable time.

Alice asked them all to excuse her for a moment while she went up to her room. Once there, she lit a piece of candle and burned the lice off the seams of the mask. She put it over her head. It did not disarrange her hair, the neat smooth hair of a minister's daughter, always presentable on any occasion. But the eyeholes came too low down, so that she could see nothing and stood there in stifling darkness. She asked herself, 'Wherein have I sinned?'

Her father, who never raised his voice, called from downstairs, 'My dear, we are waiting.' She took off the mask, folded it, and put it in the hamper where she kept her woollen stockings.

After grace they ate red snapper, boiled mutton and bread pudding, no vegetables. In England the Reverend Alfred Godley had kept a good kitchen garden, but so far he had not been able to get either leeks or cabbages going in the thin earth round Battery Point.

Mr Luke hoped that Miss Alice had found her time at the instrument well spent.

'I could not get much done,' she answered. 'I was interrupted.'

'Ah, it's a sad thing for a performer to be interrupted. The concentration of the mind is gone. "When the lamp is shattered . . ."'

'That is not what I felt at all,' said Alice.

'You are too modest to admit it.'

'I have been thinking, Father,' said Alice, 'that since Mr Luke cares so much for music, it would be a good thing for him to try the seraphine himself. Then if by any chance I had to go away, you would be sure of a replacement.'

'You speak as if my wife and I should be here always,' cried Mr Luke.

Nobody made any comment on this — certainly not Mrs Luke, who passed her days in a kind of incredulous stupor. How could it be that she was sitting here eating bread pudding some twelve thousand miles from Clerkenwell, where she had spent all the rest of her life? The Rector's attention had been drawn away by the visiting preacher, who had taken out a copy of the *Hobart Town Daily Courier*, and was reading aloud a paragraph which announced his arrival from Melbourne. 'Bringing your welcome with you,' the Rector exclaimed. 'I am glad the *Courier* noted it.' — 'Oh, they would not have done,' said the preacher, 'but I make it my practice to call in at the principal newspaper offices wherever I go, and make myself known with a few friendly words. In that way, if the editor has nothing of great moment to fill up his sheet, which is frequently the case, it is more than likely that he will include something about my witness.' He had come on a not very successful mission to pray that gold would never be discovered in Van Diemen's Land, as it had been on the mainland, bringing with it the occasion of new temptations.

After the dishes were cleared Alice said she was going back for a while to Aggie's, but would, of course, be home before dark. Mr Luke, while his wife sat on with half-closed eyes, came out to the back kitchen and asked Mrs Watson, who was at the sink, whether he could make himself useful by pumping up some more water.

'No,' said Mrs Watson.

Mr Luke persevered. 'I believe you to have had considerable experience of life. Now, I find Miss Alice charming, but somewhat difficult to understand. Will you tell me something about her?'

'No.'

Mrs Watson was, at the best of times, a very silent woman, whose life had been an unfortunate one. She had lost three children before being transported, and could not now remember what they had been called. Alice, however, did not altogether believe this, as she had met other women who thought it unlucky to name their dead children. Mrs Watson had certainly been out of luck with her third, a baby, who had been left in the charge of a

THE MEANS OF ESCAPE

little girl of ten, a neighbour's daughter, who acted as nursemaid for fourpence a week. How the house came to catch fire was not known. It was a flash fire. Mrs Watson was out at work. The man she lived with was in the house, but he was very drunk, and doing – she supposed – the best he could under the circumstances, he pitched both the neighbour's girl and the baby out of the window. The coroner had said that it might just as well have been a Punch and Judy show. 'Try to think no more about it,' Alice advised her. As chance would have it, Mrs Watson had been taken up only a week later for thieving. She had tried to throw herself in the river, but the traps had pulled her out again.

On arrival in Hobart she had been sent to the Female Factory, and later, after a year's steady conduct, to the Hiring Depot where employers could select a pass-holder. That was how, several years ago, she had fetched up at the Rectory. Alice had taught her to write and read, and had given her (as employers were required to do in any case) a copy of the Bible. She handed over the book with a kiss. On the flyleaf she had copied out a verse from Hosea – 'Say to your sister, *Ruhaman*, you have obtained mercy.'

Mrs Watson had no documents which indicated her age, and her pale face was not so much seamed or lined as knocked, apparently, out of the true by a random blow which might have been time or chance. Perhaps she had always looked like that. Although she said nothing by way of thanks at the time, it was evident, as the months

went by, that she had transferred the weight of unex-
pended affection which is one of a woman's greatest incon-
veniences on to Miss Alice. This was clear partly from the
way she occasionally caught hold of Alice's hand and
held it for a while, and from her imitation, sometimes
unconsciously grotesque, of Alice's rapid walk and her
way of doing things about the house.

Aggie had the tea, the bacon, the plum jam, and, on her
own initiative, had added a roll of tobacco. This was the
only item from the bond store and perhaps should have
been left alone, but neither of the girls had ever met or
heard of a man who didn't smoke or chew tobacco if he
had the opportunity. They knew that on Norfolk Island
and at Port Arthur the convicts sometimes killed for
tobacco.

They had a note of the exact cash value of what was
taken. Alice would repay the amount to Shuckburgh's
Hotel from the money she earned from giving music
lessons. (She had always refused to take a fee for playing
the seraphine at St George's.) But what of truth's claim,
what of honesty's? Well, Alice would leave, say, a hundred
and twenty days for *Constancy* to reach Portsmouth. Then
she would go to her father.

'What will you say to him?' Aggie asked.

'I shall tell him that I have stolen and lied, and caused
my friend to steal and lie.'

'Yes, but that was all in the name of the corporeal

mercies. You felt pity for this man, who had been a prisoner, and was alone in the wide world.'

'I am not sure that what I feel is pity.'

Certainly the two of them must have been seen through the shining front windows of the new terraced houses on their way up to the church. Certainly they were seen with their handcart, but this was associated with parish magazines and requests for a subscription to something or other, so that at the sight of it the watchers left their windows. At the top of the rise Aggie, who was longing to have a look at Alice's lag, said, 'I'll not come in with you.'

'But, Aggie, you've done so much, and you'll want to see his face.'

'I do want to see his face, but I'm keeping myself in check. That's what forms the character, keeping yourself in check at times.'

'Your character is formed already, Aggie.'

'Sakes, Alice, do you want me to come in with you?'

'No.'

'Mr Savage,' she called out decisively.

'I am just behind you.'

Without turning round, she counted out the packages in their stout wrapping of whitish paper. He did not take them, not even the tobacco, but said, 'I have been watching you and the other young lady from the tower.'

'This situation can't continue,' said Alice. 'There is the regular Moonah Men's prayer meeting on Friday.'

'I shall make a run for it tomorrow night,' said Savage,

'but I need women's clothing. I am not of heavy build. The flesh came off me at Port Arthur, one way and another. Can you furnish me?'

'I must not bring women's clothes to the church,' said Alice. 'St Paul forbids it.' But she had often felt that she was losing patience with St Paul.

'If he won't let you come to me, I must come to you,' said Savage.

'You mean to my father's house?'

'Tell me the way exactly, Miss Alice, and which your room is. As soon as the time's right, I will knock twice on your window.'

'You will not knock on it once!' said Alice. 'I don't sleep on the ground floor.'

'Does your room face the sea?'

'No, I don't care to look at the sea. My window looks on to the Derwent, up the river valley to the north-west.'

Now that she was looking at him he put his two thumbs and forefingers together in a sign which she had understood and indeed used herself ever since she was a child. It meant *I give you my whole heart.*

'I should have thought you might have wanted to know what I was going to do when I reached England,' he said.

'I do know. You'll be found out, taken up and committed to Pentonville as an escaped felon.'

'Only give me time, Miss Alice, and I will send for you.'

In defiance of any misfortune that might come to him,

he would send her the needful money for her fare and his address, once he had a home for her, in England.

'Wait and trust, give me time, and I will send for you.'

In low-built, shipshape Battery Point the Rectory was unusual in being three storeys high, but it had been smartly designed with ironwork Trafalgar balconies, and the garden had been planted with English roses as well as daisy bushes and silver wattle. It was the Rector's kind-heartedness which had made it take on the appearance of a human warren. Alice's small room, as she had told Savage, looked out on to the river. Next to her, on that side of the house, was the visiting preacher's room, always called, as in the story of Elijah, the prophet's chamber. The Lukes faced the sea, and the Rector had retreated to what had once been his study. Mrs Watson slept at the back, over the wash-house, which projected from the kitchen. Above were the box-rooms, all inhabited by a changing population of no-hopers, thrown out of work by the depression of the 1840s. These people did not eat at the Rectory — they went to the Colonial Families' Charitable on Knopwood Street — but their washing and their poultry had given the grass plot the air of a seedy encampment, ready to surrender at the first emergency.

Alice did not undress the following night, but lay down in her white blouse and waist. One of her four shawls and one of her three skirts lay folded over the back of the sewing chair. At first she lay there and smiled, then almost laughed out loud at the notion of Savage, like a mummer in a Christmas pantomime, struggling down the Battery steps and on to the wharves under the starlight in her nankeen petticoat. Then she ceased smiling, partly because she felt the unkindness of it, partly because of her perplexity as to why he needed to make this very last part of his run in skirts. Did he have in mind to set sail as a woman?

She let her thoughts run free. She knew perfectly well that Savage, after years of enforced solitude, during which he had been afforded no prospect of a woman's love, was unlikely to be coming to her room just for a bundle of clothes. If he wanted to get into bed with her, what then, ought she to raise the house? She imagined calling out (though not until he was gone), and her door opening, and the bare shanks of the rescuers jostling in in their nightshirts – the visiting preacher, Mr Luke, her father, the upstairs lodgers – and she prayed for grace. She thought of the forgiven – Rahab, the harlot of Jericho, the wife of Hosea who had been a prostitute, Mary Magdalene, Mrs Watson who had cohabited with a drunken man.

You may call me Miss Alice.

I will send for you.

You could not hear St George's clock from the Rectory. She marked the hours from the clock at Government House on the waterfront. It had been built by convict labour and intended first of all as the Customs House. It was now three o'clock. The *Constancy* sailed at first light.

Give me time and I will send for you.

If he had been seen leaving the church, and arrested, they would surely have come to tell the Rector. If he had missed the way to the Rectory and been caught wandering in the streets, then no one else was to blame but herself. I should have brought him straight home with me. He should have obtained mercy. I should have called out aloud to every one of them – look at him, this is the man who will send for me.

The first time she heard a tap at the window she lay still, thinking, 'He may look for me if he chooses.' It was nothing, there was no one there. The second and third times, at which she got up and crossed the cold floor, were also nothing.

Alice, however, did receive a letter from Savage (he still gave himself that name). It arrived about eight months later, and had been despatched from Portsmouth. By that time she was exceedingly busy, since Mrs Watson had left the Rectory, and had not been replaced.

Honoured Miss Alice,

I think it only proper to do Justice to Myself, by telling you the Circumstances which took place on the 12 of November Last Year. In the First Place, I shall not forget your Kindness. Even when I go down to the Dust, as we all shall do so, a Spark will proclaim, that Miss Alice Godley Relieved me in my Distress.

Having got to the Presbittery in accordance with your Directions, I made sure first of your Room, facing North West, and got up the House the handiest way, by scaleing the Wash-house Roof, intending to make the Circuit of the House by means of the Ballcony and its varse Quantity of creepers. But I was made to Pause at once by a Window opening and an Ivory Form leaning out, and a Woman's Voice suggesting a natural Proceeding between us, which there is no need to particularise. When we had done our business, she said further, You may call me Mrs Watson, tho it is not my Name. – I said to her, I am come here in search of Women's Clothing. I am a convict on the bolt, and it is my intention to conceal myself on Constancy, laying at Franklyn Wharf. She replied immediately, 'I can Furnish you, and indeed I can see No Reason, why I should not Accompany you.'

This letter of Savage's in its complete form, is now, like so many memorials of convict days, in the National Library of Tasmania, in Hobart. There is no word in it to Alice Godley from Mrs Watson herself. It would seem that like many people who became literate later in life she read a great deal – the Bible in particular – but never took much to writing, and tended to mistrust it. In consequence her motives for doing what she did – which, taking into account her intense affection for Alice, must have been complex enough – were never set down, and can only be guessed at.

The Axe

The Axe

You will recall that when the planned redundancies became necessary as the result of the discouraging trading figures shown by this small firm – in contrast, so I gather from the Company reports, with several of your other enterprises – you personally deputed to me the task of 'speaking' to those who were to be asked to leave. It was suggested to me that if they were asked to resign in order to avoid the unpleasantness of being given their cards, it might be unnecessary for the firm to offer any compensation. Having glanced personally through my staff sheets, you underlined the names of four people, the first being that of my clerical assistant, W. S. Singlebury. Your actual words to me were that he seemed fairly old and could probably be frightened into taking a powder. You were speaking to me in your 'democratic' style.

From this point on I feel able to write more freely, it being well understood, at office-managerial level, that you do not read more than the first two sentences of any given report. You believe that anything which cannot be put into two sentences is not worth attending to, a piece of wisdom which you usually attribute to the late Lord Beaverbrook.

As I question whether you have ever seen Singlebury, with whom this report is mainly concerned, it may be helpful to describe him. He worked for the Company for many more years than myself, and his attendance record was excellent. On Mondays, Wednesdays and Fridays, he wore a blue suit and a green knitted garment with a front zip. On Tuesdays and Thursdays he wore a pair of grey trousers of man-made material which he called 'my flannels', and a fawn cardigan. The cardigan was omitted in summer. He had, however, one distinguishing feature, very light blue eyes, with a defensive expression, as though apologizing for something which he felt guilty about, but could not put right. The fact is that he was getting old. Getting old is, of course, a crime of which we grow more guilty every day.

Singlebury had no wife or dependants, and was by no means a communicative man. His room is, or was, a kind of cubby-hole adjoining mine − you have to go through it to get into my room − and it was always kept very neat. About his 'things' he did show some mild emotion. They had to be ranged in a certain pattern in respect to his in and out trays, and Singlebury stayed behind for two or three minutes every evening to do this. He also managed to retain every year the complimentary desk calendar sent to us by Dino's, the Italian cafe on the corner. Singlebury was in fact the only one of my personnel who was always quite certain of the date. To this too his attitude was apologetic. His phrase was, 'I'm afraid it's Tuesday'.

His work, as was freely admitted, was his life, but the nature of his duties – though they included the post-book and the addressograph – was rather hard to define, having grown round him with the years. I can only say that after he left, I was surprised myself to discover how much he had had to do.

Oddly connected in my mind with the matter of the redundancies is the irritation of the damp in the office this summer and the peculiar smell (not the ordinary smell of damp), emphasized by the sudden appearance of representatives of a firm of damp eliminators who had not been sent for by me, nor is there any record of my having done so. These people simply vanished at the end of the day and have not returned. Another firm, to whom I applied as a result of frequent complaints by the female staff, have answered my letters but have so far failed to call.

Singlebury remained unaffected by the smell. Joining, very much against his usual habit, in one of the too frequent discussions of the subject, he said that he knew what it was; it was the smell of disappointment. For an awkward moment I thought he must have found out by some means that he was going to be asked to go, but he went on to explain that in 1942 the whole building had been requisitioned by the Admiralty and that relatives had been allowed to wait or queue there in the hope of getting news of those missing at sea. The repeated disappointment of these women, Singlebury said, must have permeated the building like a corrosive gas. All this was very unlike him. I made it a point not to encourage anything morbid. Singlebury was quite insistent, and added, as though by way of proof, that the lino in the corridors was Admiralty issue and had not been renewed since 1942 either. I was astonished to realize that he had been working in the building for so many years before the present tenancy. I realized that he must be considerably older than he had given us to understand. This, of course, will mean that there are wrong entries on his cards.

The actual notification to the redundant staff passed off rather better, in a way, than I had anticipated. By that time everyone in the office seemed inexplicably conversant with the details, and several of them in fact had gone far beyond their terms of reference, young Patel, for instance, who openly admits that he will be leaving us as soon as he can get a better job, taking me aside and telling me that to such a man as Singlebury dismissal would be like death. Dismissal is not the right word, I said. But death is, Patel replied. Singlebury himself, however, took it very quietly. Even when I raised the question of the Company's Early Retirement pension scheme, which I could not pretend was over-generous, he said very little. He was generally felt to be in a state of shock. The two girls whom you asked me to speak to were quite unaffected, having already found themselves employments as host-esses at the Dolphinarium near here. Mrs Horrocks, of

Filing, on the other hand, *did* protest, and was so offensive on the question of severance pay that I was obliged to agree to refer it to a higher level. I consider this as one of the hardest day's work that I have ever done for the Company.

Just before his month's notice (if we are to call it that) was up, Singlebury, to my great surprise, asked me to come home with him one evening for a meal. In all the past years the idea of his having a home, still less asking anyone back to it, had never arisen, and I did not at all want to go there now. I felt sure, too, that he would want to reopen the matter of compensation, and only a quite unjustified feeling of guilt made me accept. We took an Underground together after work, travelling in the late rush-hour to Clapham North, and walked some distance in the rain. His place, when we eventually got to it, seemed particularly inconvenient, the entrance being through a small cleaner's shop. It consisted of one room and a shared toilet on the half-landing. The room itself was tidy, arranged, so it struck me, much on the lines of his cubby-hole, but the window was shut and it was oppressively stuffy. This is where I bury myself, said Singlebury.

There were no cooking arrangements and he left me there while he went down to fetch us something ready to eat from the Steakorama next to the cleaner's. In his absence I took the opportunity to examine his room, though of course not in an inquisitive or prying manner. I was struck by the fact that none of his small store of stationery had been brought home from the office. He returned with two steaks wrapped in aluminium foil, evidently a special treat in my honour, and afterwards he went out on to the landing and made cocoa, a drink which I had not tasted for more than thirty years. The evening dragged rather. In the course of conversation it turned out that Singlebury was fond of reading. There were in fact several issues of a colour-printed encyclopaedia which he had been collecting as it came out, but unfortunately it had ceased publication after the seventh part. Reading is my hobby, he said. I pointed out that a hobby was rather something that one did with one's hands or in the open air — a relief from the work of the brain. Oh, I don't accept that distinction, Singlebury said. The mind and the body are the same. Well, one cannot deny the connection, I replied. Fear, for example, releases adrenalin, which directly affects the nerves. I don't mean connection, I mean identity, Singlebury said, the mind is the blood. Nonsense, I said, you might just as well tell me that the blood is the mind. It stands to reason that the blood can't think.

I was right, after all, in thinking that he would refer to the matter of the redundancy. This was not till he was seeing me off at the bus-stop, when for a moment he turned his grey, exposed-looking face away from me and said that he did not see how he could manage if he really had to go. He stood there like someone who has 'tried to give satisfaction' — he even used this phrase, saying that if the expression were not redolent of a bygone age, he would like to feel he had given satisfaction. Fortunately we had not long to wait for the 45 bus.

At the expiry of the month the staff gave a small tea-party for those who were leaving. I cannot describe this occasion as a success.

The following Monday I missed Singlebury as a familiar presence and also, as mentioned above, because I had never quite realized how much work he had been taking upon himself. As a direct consequence of losing him I found myself having to stay late – not altogether unwillingly, since although following general instructions I have discouraged overtime, the extra pay in my own case would be instrumental in making ends meet. Meanwhile Singlebury's desk had not been cleared – that is, of the trays, pencil-sharpener and complimentary calendar which were, of course, office property. The feeling that he would come back – not like Mrs Horrocks, who has rung up and called round incessantly – but simply come back to work out of habit and through not knowing what else to do, was very strong, without being openly mentioned. I myself half expected and dreaded it, and I had mentally prepared two or three lines of argument in order to persuade him, if he *did* come, not to try it again. Nothing happened, however, and on the Thursday I personally removed the 'things' from the cubby-hole into my own room.

Meanwhile in order to dispel certain quite unfounded rumours I thought it best to issue a notice for general circulation, pointing out that if Mr Singlebury should turn out to have taken any unwise step, and if in consequence any inquiry should be necessary, we should be the first to hear about it from the police. I dictated this to our only permanent typist, who immediately said, oh, he would never do that. He would never cause any unpleasantness like bringing police into the place, he'd do all he could to avoid that. I did not encourage any further discussion, but I asked my wife, who is very used to social work, to call round at Singlebury's place in Clapham North and find out how he was. She did not have very much luck. The people in the cleaner's shop knew, or thought they knew, that he was away, but they had not been sufficiently interested to ask where he was going.

On Friday young Patel said he would be leaving, as the damp and the smell were affecting his health. The damp is certainly not drying out in this seasonably warm weather.

I also, as you know, received another invitation on the Friday, at very short notice, in fact no notice at all; I was told to come to your house in Suffolk Park Gardens that evening for drinks. I was not unduly elated, having been asked once before after I had done rather an awkward small job for you. In our Company, justice has not only have not to be done, but it must be seen not to be done. The food was quite nice; it came from your Caterers Grade 3. I spent most of the evening talking to Ted Hollow, one of the area sales-managers. I did not expect to be introduced to your wife, nor was I. Towards the end of the evening you spoke to me for three minutes in the small room with a green marble floor and matching wallpaper leading to the ground-floor toilets. You asked me if everything was all right, to which I replied, all right for whom? You said that nobody's fault was nobody's funeral. I said that I had tried to give satisfaction. Passing on towards the washbasins, you told me with seeming cordiality to be careful and watch it when I had had mixed drinks.

I would describe my feeling at this point as resentment, and I cannot identify exactly the moment when it passed into unease. I do know that I was acutely uneasy as I crossed the hall and saw two of your domestic staff, a man and a woman, holding my coat, which I had left in the lobby, and apparently trying to brush it. Your domestic staff all appear to be of foreign extraction and I personally feel sorry for them and do not grudge them a smile at the oddly assorted guests. Then I saw they were not smiling at my coat but that they seemed to be examining their fingers and looking at me earnestly and silently, and the collar or shoulders of my coat was covered with blood. As I came up to them, although they were still both absolutely silent, the illusion or impression passed, and I put on my coat and left the house in what I hope was a normal manner.

I now come to the present time. The feeling of uneasiness which I have described as making itself felt in your house has not diminished during this past weekend, and partly to take my mind off it and partly for the reasons I have given, I decided to work over-time again tonight,

Monday the twenty-third. This was in spite of the fact that the damp smell had become almost a stench, as of something putrid, which must have affected my nerves to some extent, because when I went out to get something to eat at Dino's I left the lights on, both in my own office and in the entrance hall. I mean that for the first time since I began to work for the Company I left them on deliberately. As I walked to the corner I looked back and saw the two solitary lights looking somewhat forlorn in contrast to the glitter of the Arab-American Mutual Loan Corporation opposite. After my meal I felt absolutely reluctant to go back to the building, and wished then that I had not given way to the impulse to leave the lights on, but since I had done so and they must be turned off, I had no choice.

As I stood in the empty hallway I could hear the numerous creakings, settlings and faint tickings of an old building, possibly associated with the plumbing system. The lifts for reasons of economy do not operate after 6.30 p.m., so I began to walk up the stairs. After one flight I felt a strong creeping tension in the nerves of the back such as any of us feel when there is danger from behind; one might say that the body was thinking for itself on these occasions. I did not look round, but simply continued upwards as rapidly as I could. At the third floor I paused, and could hear footsteps coming patiently up behind me. This was not a surprise; I had been expecting them all evening.

Just at the door of my own office, or rather of the

cubby-hole, for I have to pass through that, I turned, and saw at the end of the dim corridor what I had also expected, Singlebury, advancing towards me with his unmistakable shuffling step. My first reaction was a kind of bewilderment as to why he, who had been such an excellent timekeeper, so regular day by day, should become a creature of the night. He was wearing the blue suit. This I could make out by its familiar outline, but it was not till he came halfway down the corridor towards me, and reached the patch of light falling through the window from the street, that I saw that he was not himself – I mean that his head was nodding or rather swivelling irregularly from side to side. It crossed my mind that Singlebury was drunk. I had never known him drunk or indeed seen him take anything to drink, even at the office Christmas party, but one cannot estimate the effect that trouble will have upon a man. I began to think what steps I should take in this situation. I turned on the light in his cubby-hole as I went through and waited at the entrance of my own office. As he appeared in the outer doorway I saw that I had not been correct about the reason for the odd movement of the head. The throat was cut from ear to ear so that the head was nearly severed from the shoulders. It was this which had given the impression of nodding, or rather, lolling. As he walked into his cubby-hole Singlebury raised both hands and tried to steady the head as though conscious that something was wrong. The eyes were thickly filmed over, as one sees in the carcasses in a butcher's shop.

I shut and locked my door, and not wishing to give way to nausea, or to lose all control of myself, I sat down at my desk. My work was waiting for me as I had left it – it was the file on the matter of the damp elimination – and, there not being anything else to do, I tried to look through it. On the other side of the door I could hear Singlebury sit down also, and then try the drawers of the table, evidently looking for the 'things' without which he could not start work. After the drawers had been tried, one after another, several times, there was almost total silence.

The present position is that I am locked in my own office and would not, no matter what you offered me, indeed I could not, go out through the cubby-hole and pass what is sitting at the desk. The early cleaners will not be here for seven hours and forty-five minutes. I have passed the time so far as best I could in writing this report. One consideration strikes me. If what I have next door is a visitant which should not be walking but buried in the earth, then its wound cannot bleed, and there will be no stream of blood moving slowly under the whole width of the communicating door. However I am sitting at the moment with my back to the door, so that, without turning round, I have no means of telling whether it has done so or not.

The Red-Haired Girl

The Red-Haired Girl

Hackett, Holland, Parsons, Charrington and Dubois all studied in Paris, in the atelier of Vincent Bonvin. Dubois, although his name sounded French, wasn't, and didn't speak any either. None of them did except Hackett.

In the summer of 1882 they made up a party to go to Brittany. That was because they admired Bastien-Lepage, which old Bonvin certainly didn't, and because they wanted somewhere cheap, somewhere with characteristic types, absolutely natural, busy with picturesque occupations, and above all, plein air. 'Your work cannot be really good unless you have caught a cold doing it,' said Hackett.

They were poor enough, but they took a certain quantity of luggage — only the necessities. Their canvases needed rigging like small craft putting out of harbour, and the artists themselves, for plein air work, had brought overcoats, knickerbockers, gaiters, boots, wide-awakes, broad straw hats for sunny days. They tried, to begin with, St Briac-sur-Mer, which had been recommended to them in Paris, but it didn't suit. On, then, to Palourde, on the coast near Cancale. All resented the time spent moving about. It wasn't in the spirit of the thing, they were artists, not sightseers.

At Palourde, although it looked, and was, larger than St Briac, there was, if anything, less room. The Palourdais had never come across artists before, considered them as rich rather than poor, and wondered why they did not go to St Malo. Holland, Parsons, Charrington and Dubois, however, each found a room of sorts. What about their possessions? There were sail-lofts and potato-cellars in Palourde, but, it seemed, not an inch of room to spare. Their clothes, books and painting material had to go in some boats pulled up above the foreshore, awaiting repairs. They were covered with a piece of tarred sailcloth and roped down. Half the morning would have to be spent getting out what was wanted. Hackett, as interpreter, was obliged to ask whether there was any risk of their being stolen. The reply was that no one in Palourde wanted such things.

It was agreed that Hackett should take what appeared to be the only room in the constricted Hôtel du Port. 'Right under the rafters,' he wrote to his Intended, 'a bed, a chair, a basin, a *broc* of cold water brought up once a day, no view from the window, but I shan't of course paint in my room anyway. I have propped up the canvases I brought with me against the wall. That gives me the sensation of having done something. The food, so far, you wouldn't approve of. Black porridge, later on pieces of black porridge left over from the morning and fried, fish soup with onions, onion soup with fish. The thing is to understand these people well, try to share their devotion to onions, and above all to secure a good model –' He decided not to add 'who must be a young girl, otherwise I haven't much chance of any of the London exhibitions.'

The Hôtel du Port was inconveniently placed at the top of the village. It had no restaurant, but Hackett was told that he could be served, if he wanted it, at half past six o'clock. The ground floor was taken up with the bar, so this service would be in a very small room at the back, opening off the kitchen.

After Hackett had sat for some time at a narrow table covered with rose-patterned oilcloth, the door opened sufficiently for a second person to edge into the room. It was a red-haired girl, built for hard use and hard wear, who without speaking put down a bowl of fish soup. She and the soup between them filled the room with a sharp, cloudy odour, not quite disagreeable, but it wasn't possible for her to get in and out, concentrating always on not spilling anything, without knocking the back of the chair and the door itself, first with her elbows, then with her rump. The spoons and the saltbox on the table trembled as though in a railway carriage. Then the same manoeuvre again, this time bringing a loaf of dark bread and a carafe of cider. No more need to worry after that, there was no more to come.

'I think I've found rather a jolly-looking model already,' Hackett told the others. They, too, had not done so badly. They had set up their easels on the quay, been asked, as far as they could make out, to move them further away from the moorings, done so 'with a friendly smile,' said Charrington — 'we find that goes a long way.' They hadn't risked asking anyone to model for them, just started some sea-pieces between the handfuls of wind and rain. 'We might come up to the hotel tonight and dine with you. There's nothing but fish soup in our digs.'

Hackett discouraged them.

The hotelier's wife, when he had made the right pre-liminary enquiries from her about the red-haired girl, had answered — as she did, however, on all subjects — largely with silences. He didn't learn who her parents were, or even her family name. Her given name was Annik. She worked an all-day job at the Hôtel du Port, but she had one and a half hours free after her lunch and if she wanted to spend that being drawn or painted, well, there were no objections. Not in the hotel, however, where, as he could see, there was no room.

'I paint en plein air,' said Hackett.

'You'll find plenty of that.'

'I shall pay her, of course.'

'You must make your own arrangements.'

He spoke to the girl at dinner, during the few moments when she was conveniently trapped. When she had quite skilfully allowed the door to shut behind her and, soup-dish in hand, was recovering her balance, he said:

'Anny, I want to ask you something.'

'I'm called Annik,' she said. It was the first time he had heard her speak.

'All the girls are called that. I shall call you Anny. I've spoken about you to the patronne.'

'Yes, she told me.'

Anny was a heavy breather, and the whole tiny room seemed to expand and deflate as she stood pondering.

'I shall want you to come to the back door of the hotel, I mean the back steps down to the rue de Dol. Let us say tomorrow, at twelve forty-five.'

'I don't know about the forty-five,' she said. 'I can't be sure about that.'

'How do you usually know the time?' She was silent. He thought it was probably a matter of pride and she did not want to agree to anything too easily. But possibly she couldn't tell the time. She might be stupid to the degree of idiocy.

The Hôtel du Port had no courtyard. Like every other house in the street, it had a flight of stone steps to adapt to the change of level. After lunch the shops shut for an hour and the women of Palourde sat or stood, according to their age, on the top step and knitted or did crochet. They didn't wear costume any more, they wore white linen caps and jackets, long skirts, and, if they weren't going far, carpet slippers.

Anny was punctual to the minute. 'I shall want you to stand quite still on the top step, with your back to the door. I've asked them not to open it.'

Anny, also, was wearing carpet slippers. 'I can't just stand here doing nothing.'

He allowed her to fetch her crochet. Give a little, take a little. He was relieved, possibly a bit disappointed, to find how little interest they caused in the rue de Dol. He was used to being watched, quite openly, over his shoulder, as if he was giving a comic performance. Here even the children didn't stop to look.

'They don't care about our picture,' he said, trying to amuse her. He would have liked a somewhat gentler expression. Certainly she was not a beauty. She hadn't the white skin of the dreamed-of red-haired girl, in fact her face and neck were covered with a faint but noticeable hairy down, as though proof against all weathers.

'How long will it take?' she asked.

'I don't know. As God disposes! An hour will do for today.'

'And then you'll pay me?'

'No,' he said, 'I shan't do that. I shall pay you when the whole thing's finished. I shall keep a record of the time you've worked, and if you like you can keep one as well.'

As he was packing up his box of charcoals he added: 'I shall want to make a few colour notes tomorrow, and I should like you to wear a red shawl.' It seemed that she hadn't one. 'But you could borrow one, my dear. You could borrow one, since I ask you particularly.'

She looked at him as though he were an imbecile.

'You shouldn't have said "Since I ask you particularly",' Parsons told him that evening. 'That will have turned her head.'

'It can't have done,' said Hackett.

'Did you call her "my dear"?'

'I don't know, I don't think so.'

'I've noticed you say "particularly" with a peculiar intonation, which may well have become a matter of habit,' said Parsons, nodding sagely.

This is driving me crazy, thought Hackett. He began to feel a division which he had never so much as dreamed of in Paris between himself and his fellow students. They had been working all day, having managed to rent a disused and indeed almost unusable shed on the quay. It had once been part of the market where the fishermen's wives did the triage, sorting out the catch by size. Hackett, as before, had done the interpreting. He had plenty of time, since Anny could only be spared for such short intervals. But at least he had been true to his principles. Holland, Parsons, Charrington and Dubois weren't working in the open air at all. Difficulties about models forgotten, they were sketching each other in the shed. The background of Palourde's not very picturesque jetty could be dashed in later.

Anny appeared promptly for the next three days to stand, with her crochet, on the back steps. Hackett didn't mind her blank expression, having accepted from the first that she was never likely to smile. The red shawl, though — that hadn't appeared. He could, perhaps, buy one in St Malo. He ached for the contrast between the copper-coloured hair and the scarlet shawl. But he felt it wrong to introduce something from outside Palourde.

'Anny, I have to tell you that you've disappointed me.'

'I told you I had no red shawl.'

'You could have borrowed one.'

Charrington, who was supposed to understand women, and even to have had a great quarrel with Parsons about some woman or other, only said: 'She can't borrow what isn't there. I've been trying ever since we came here to borrow a decent tin-opener. I've tried to make it clear that I'd give it back.'

Best to leave the subject alone. But the moment Anny turned up next day he found himself saying: 'You could borrow one from a friend, that was what I meant.'

'I haven't any friends,' said Anny.

Hackett paused in the business of lighting his pipe. 'An empty life for you, then, Anny.'

'You don't know what I want,' she said, very low.

'Oh, everybody wants the same things. The only differ-
ence is what they will do to get them.'

'You don't know what I want, and you don't know
what I feel,' she said, still in the same mutter. There
was, however, a faint note of something more than the
contradiction that came so naturally to her, and Hackett
was a good-natured man.

'I'm sorry I said you disappointed me, Anny. The truth
is I find it rather a taxing business, standing here drawing
in the street.'

'I don't know why you came here in the first place.
There's nothing here, nothing at all. If it's oysters you
want, they're better at Cancale. There's nothing here
to tell one morning from another, except to see if it's
raining . . . Once they brought in three drowned bodies,
two men and a boy, a whole boat's crew, and laid them
out on the tables in the fish market, and you could see
blood and water running out of their mouths . . . You
can spend your whole life here, wash, pray, do your work,
and all the time you might just as well not have been
born.'

She was still speaking so that she could scarcely be heard.
The passers-by went un-noticing down Palourde's badly
paved street. Hackett felt disturbed. It had never occurred
to him that she would speak, without prompting, at such
length.

*   *   *

'I've received a telegram from Paris,' said Parsons, who was standing at the shed door. 'It's taken its time about getting here. They gave it me at the post office.'

'What does it say?' asked Hackett, feeling it was likely to be about money.

'Well, that he's coming — Bonvin, I mean. As is my custom every summer, I am touring the coasts — it's a kind of informal inspection, you see. — Expect me, then, on the 27th for dinner at the Hôtel du Port.'

'It's impossible.' Parsons suggested that, since Dubois had brought his banjo with him, they might get up some kind of impromptu entertainment. But he had to agree that one couldn't associate old Bonvin with entertainment.

He couldn't, surely, be expected from Paris before six. But when they arrived, all of them except Hackett carrying their portfolios, at the hotel's front door, they recognized, from the moment it opened, the voice of Bonvin. Hackett looked round, and felt his head swim. The bar, dark, faded, pickled in its own long-standing odours, crowded with stools and barrels, with the air of being older than Palourde, as though Palourde had been built round it without daring to disturb it, was swept and emptied now except for a central table and chairs such as Hackett had never seen in the hotel. At the head of the table sat old Bonvin. 'Sit down, gentlemen! I am your host!' The everyday malicious dry voice, but a different Bonvin, in splendid seaside dress, a yellow waistcoat, a cravat. Palourde was indifferent to artists, but Bonvin had imposed himself as a professor.

'They are used to me here. They keep a room for me which I think is not available to other guests and they are always ready to take a little trouble for me when I come.'

The artists sat meekly down, while the patronne herself served them with a small glass of greenish-white muscadet.

'I am your host,' repeated Bonvin. 'I can only say that I am delighted to see pupils, for the first time, in Palourde, but I assure you I have others as far away as Corsica. Once a teacher, always a teacher! I sometimes think it is a passion which outlasts even art itself.'

They had all assured each other, in Paris, that old Bonvin was incapable of teaching anything. Time spent in his atelier was squandered. But here, in the strangely transformed bar of the Hôtel du Port, with a quite inadequate drink in front of them, they felt overtaken by destiny. The patronne shut and locked the front door to keep out the world who might disturb the professor. Bonvin, not, after all, looking so old, called upon them to show their portfolios.

Hackett had to excuse himself to go up to his room and fetch the four drawings which he had made so far. He felt it an injustice that he had to show his things last.

Bonvin asked him to hold them up one by one, then to lay them out on the table. To Hackett he spoke magniloquently, in French.

'Yes, they are bad,' he said, 'but, M. Hackett, they are

bad for two distinct reasons. In the first place, you should not draw the view from the top of a street if you cannot manage the perspective, which even a child, following simple mechanical rules, can do. The relationship in scale of the main figure to those lower down is quite, quite wrong. But there is something else amiss.

'You are an admirer, I know, of Bastien-Lepage, who has said, "There is nothing really lasting, nothing that will endure, except the sincere expression of the actual conditions of life." Conditions in the potato patch, in the hayfield, at the washtub, in the open street! That is pernicious nonsense. Look at this girl of yours. Evidently she is not a professional model, for she doesn't know how to hold herself. I see you have made a note that the colour of the hair is red, but that is the only thing I know about her. She's standing against the door like a beast waiting to be put back in its stall. It's your intention, I am sure, to do the finished version in the same way, in the dust of the street. Well, your picture will say nothing and it will be nothing. It is only in the studio that you can bring out the heart of the subject, and that is what we are sent into this world to do, M. Hackett, to paint the experiences of the heart.'

(– Gibbering dotard, you can talk till your teeth fall out. I shall go on precisely as I have been doing, even if I can only paint her for an hour and a quarter a day. –) An evening of nameless embarrassment, with Hackett's friends coughing, shuffling, eating noisily, asking questions to which they knew the answer, and telling anecdotes of which they forgot the endings. Anny had not appeared, evidently she was considered unworthy; the patronne came in again, bringing not soup but the very height of Brittany's grand-occasion cuisine, a fricassee of chicken. Who would have thought there were chickens in Palourde?

Hackett woke in what he supposed were the small hours. So far he had slept dreamlessly in Palourde, had never so much as lighted his bedside candle. − Probably, he thought, Bonvin made the same unpleasant speech wherever he went. The old impostor was drunk with power − not with anything else, only half a bottle of muscadet and, later, a bottle of *gros-plant* between the six of them. − The sky had begun to thin and pale. It came to him that what had been keeping him awake was not an injustice of Bonvin's, but of his own. What had been the experiences of Anny's heart?

Bonvin, with his dressing cases and book-boxes, left early. The horse omnibus stopped once a week in the little Place François-René de Chateaubriand, at the entrance to the village. Having made his formal farewells, Bonvin caught the omnibus. Hackett was left in good time for his appointment with Anny.

She did not come that day, nor the next day, nor the day after. On the first evening he was served by the boot-boy, pitifully worried about getting in and out of the door, on the second by the hotel laundrywoman, on the third by the patronne. 'Where is Anny?' She did not answer. For that in itself Hackett was prepared, but he tried again. 'Is she ill?' 'No, not ill.' 'Has she taken another job?' 'No.' He was beginning, he realized, in the matter of this plain and sullen girl, to sound like an anxious lover. 'Shall I see her again?' He got no answer.

Had she drowned herself? The question reared up in his mind, like a savage dog getting up from its sleep. She had hardly seemed to engage herself enough with life, hardly seemed to take enough interest in it to wish no more of it. Boredom, though, and the withering sense of insignificance can bring one as low as grief. He had felt the breath of it at his ear when Bonvin had told him — for that was what it came to — that there was no hope of his becoming an artist. Anny was stupid, but no one is too stupid to despair.

There was no police station in Palourde, and if Anny were truly drowned, they would say nothing about it at the Hôtel du Port. Hackett had been in enough small hotels to know that they did not discuss anything that was bad for business. The red-haired body might drift anywhere, might be washed ashore anywhere between Pointe du Grouin and Cap Prehel.

That night it was the laundrywoman's turn to dish up the fish soup. Hackett thought of confiding in her, but did not need to. She said to him: 'You mustn't keep asking the patronne about Anny, it disturbs her.' Anny, it turned out, had been dismissed for stealing from the hotel — some money, and a watch. 'You had better have a look through your things,' the laundrywoman said, 'and see there's nothing missing. One often doesn't notice till a good while afterwards.'

Beehernz

Beehernz

To Hopkins, deputy artistic director of the Midland Music Festival, an idea came. Not a new idea, but rather comforting in its familiarity, an idea for the two opening concerts next year. He put it forward, not at the preliminary meeting, still at quite an early one.

'Out of the question if it involves us in any further expense,' said the chairman.

'No, it's a matter of concept,' said Hopkins. 'These are Mahler concerts, agreed, and we need Mahler specialists.

'I suggest that for the first one we book a young tearaway, no shortage of those, and for the other a retired maestro – well, they don't retire, but I have in mind a figure from the past making one of his rare appearances, venerated, dug up for the occasion, someone, perhaps, thought to be dead.'

He mentioned the name of Beehernz. Most of those present had thought he was dead. Some of them remembered the name, but did not get it quite right. It was thought he had something to do with the 'Symphony of a Thousand'. In fact, however, he'd had nothing to do with it. Nearly forty years earlier, in 1960, the BBC had celebrated the centenary of Mahler's birth. It was only at a very late stage that Beehernz, booked for the occasion, had said, in his quiet way – that was how it had been described to Hopkins, 'in his quiet way' – that he would prefer a substitute to be found for him, since he had only just learned that he was expected to conduct the Eighth Symphony.

'What is your objection to the English Symphony?' he was asked.

'It is too noisy,' replied Beehernz.

Beehernz had not appeared in public since that time. Hopkins's committee agreed that his name could be made into a talking point. Would Hopkins undertake the arrangements? Yes, everything, everything.

According to the BBC's records, Beehernz lived in Scotland and had done so since 1960 – not on the mainland, but on an island off an island – Reilig, off Iona, off Mull, via Oban.

'"Reilig" means "graveyard" in Gaelic,' said the BBC reference librarian.

'There's no regular ferry from Iona,' said the Scottish Tourist Board, 'but you can enquire at Fionnphort.'

Preliminaries were conducted by letter, because Beehernz was not on the telephone. Some of Hopkins's letters were answered, in not very firm handwriting. The contract too came back, signed, but still not pleasing to the festival's accounts manager. 'Where's the compensation clause? A specific sum should be named as a guarantee of his appearance ... They can go missing at any age ... Stokowski signed a ten-year recording contract at the age of ninety-five ... It's worse as they get older, they just forget to turn up ... It needn't be an immense sum ... What does he live on, anyway?' Hopkins replied that he supposed Beehernz lived on his savings.

Hopkins was more interested in what the old maestro was going to play. Something, certainly, that wouldn't need more than two rehearsals, if possible only one.

'I'd better go and see him myself,' he said. This was what he had always had in mind.

He was going to take two other people with him. One was a singer, Mary Lockett. He didn't know her at all well, but she was only just starting on her career and wouldn't refuse – no one ever refused a free trip to Scotland. She had a 'white' voice, not really at all the kind of voice Mahler had liked himself, but she was said to be adaptable. Then he'd take his dogsbody from the festival office, young Fraser. In the evening on the Isle of Reilig they would sit round the piano and let decisions grow. Hopkins couldn't decide whether he expected to find the old man seated, solipsistic, huddled in past memories, or nervously awaiting visitors, trembling in the over-eagerness of welcome. Hopkins wrote to say they would arrive on the twenty-first of May, leaving the car in Oban.

'We'll do well to buy some supplies here,' said young Fraser. 'Mr Beehernz will very likely not have much in the house.'

They went to Oban's largest supermarket and bought tea. Celebrated Auld Style Shortbread, cold bacon, and, after some hesitation on Hopkins's part, a bottle of whisky. Half a bottle would look too calculated. He didn't know whether Mary Lockett took an occasional drink or not.

'There's always a first time,' said Fraser reassuringly.

They crossed to Mull, Fraser and Mary with their backpacks, Hopkins with his discreet travel-bag and document case. There was a message for them at Fionnphort, telling them to take the next ferry to Iona, and wait for McGregor. At Iona's jetty all the other day-trippers got out and began to walk off briskly, as though drilled, northward towards the Cathedral. Time passes more slowly in small places. After what was perhaps three-quarters of an hour, someone who was evidently McGregor came jolting towards them in a Subaru. They'd have to drive over, he said, to the west coast, where he kept his boat at moorings.

Iona is three miles long and one mile wide, and Reilig looked considerably smaller. The blue sky, cloudless that day, burned as if it was as salt as the water below them. There was no sand or white shell beach as you approached, and the rocky shoreline was not impressive, just enough to give you a nasty fall. There was a landing stage with a tarred shed beside it, and a paved track leading up to a small one-storey building of sorts.

'Is that Mr Beehernz's crofthouse?' Hopkins asked. McGregor replied that it was not a croft, but it was Beehernz's place.

'I imagine he's expecting us,' said Hopkins, although he felt it as a kind of weakness to appeal to McGregor, who told them that the door would be open and they'd best go in, but Beehernz might be there or he might be out on his potato patch. When he had seen them safely off the landing stage he disappeared into the shed, which was roofed with corrugated iron.

The front door was shut fast and weeds had grown as high as the lock. The door at the side was open, and led into a dark little hen-kitchen with just about enough room for a sink and a dresser and two dishevelled fowls who ran shrieking into the bright air outside. Fraser and Mary stood awkwardly by the sink, politeness suggesting to them to go no further.

'Beehernz!' Hopkins called. 'May we come in?'

I need absolutely to find out what he's really like. This is the opportunity before he comes back.

One step up into the living-room, white-washed, a clock ticking, no electricity, no radio, a single bed covered with a plaid, an armchair, no books, no bookcase, no scores, no manuscripts. Through into the kitchen, hardly bigger than a cupboard, a paraffin lamp waiting to be filled, a venerable bread crock, and, taking up half the space, a piano, a sad old mission-hall thing, still, a piano. Hopkins lifted the lid and tried the sagging middle C. It was silent. He played up the scale and down. No sound.

Next door, the scullery and water-closet, fit for an anti-quarian.

A disturbance in the hen-kitchen, where the two seedy fowls were rushing in again, revelling in their own panic. Mary and Fraser had just been joined by a third party, an old man who had taken off his gum-boots and was now concentrating all his attention on putting on his slippers.

'Ah, you must be . . .' said Hopkins. *But that's quite wrong. I don't want to sound as though I'm the host.*

Beehernz at length said, 'I am sorry, but you must let me rest a little. My health, such of it as remains, depends on my doing the same thing at the same time every day.'

He advanced with padding steps, a little, light old man, and sat down in the only chair. Hopkins and Fraser sat gingerly on the bed. Mary did not come into the living-room. She was still in the hen-kitchen, unfastening the backpacks and taking out the Celebrated Auld Style Short-bread, the cold bacon and the tea. She then began to take down the tin plates from the dresser. Mary never did anything in a hurry. As she moved about she could be heard singing, just quietly, from the middle of her voice, not paying any particular heed – it was a nursery tune in any case:

> 'Ich ging im Walde
> So für mich hin,
> Und nichts zu suchen,
> Das war mein Sinn.

In Schatten sah ich
Ein Blümlein stehn —
Where am I to lay out the plates?'

Beehernz was on his feet. 'No, no, not now, not yet. Not
yet. Let the young people go out for a little while.'

'But we brought . . .' Fraser said, in unconcealed disappointment.

'For a little while,' repeated Beehernz.

'Let me explain, Mr Hopkins. I would prefer Mr — er
— and Miss — er — I would prefer them to go back to Iona
with McGregor's boat. Yes, that is what I wish.'

'This is rather unexpected. I wrote to you, you remember, to tell you that there would be three of us
coming.'

Beehernz passed his hands over his forehead and looked
out from between them, as though playing some melan-
choly game.

'Three is too many, Mr Hopkins, to impose upon me
so suddenly.'

*What's come over him? He may have it in mind to push the two of
them over the cliff's edge, two souls for whom I'm responsible to the
festival committee.*

'I'll go and see where they are.'

After all, they couldn't go far. They were sitting on a
rocky outcrop, looking westward.

Fraser seemed to be silent, perhaps from hunger. Mary
never said much at any time. She was twisting the straw
handle of her shopping bag between her fingers. Why did

women always have to carry bags about with them?

Hopkins made his explanation. An old man's fancy. They mustn't, of course, take it personally.

'How else can we take it?' Fraser asked.

'You'll be able to get accommodation on Iona, perhaps at the Abbey.'

'Will there be room?'

'Well, perhaps you'll find they've taken some vow not to turn away travellers in an emergency. You must both of you get someone to sign your expenses and keep them in duplicate, of course.'

'Surely we ought to say a few words of thanks to Mr Beehernz,' said Fraser.

'No, no, you've nothing to thank him for, you'd better go and put your things together.' McGregor, indeed, was advancing up the path, saying that if there was anyone for the return journey, they would want to be getting into the boat.

As the boat ticked away through the calm and sparkling water, Fraser seemed to be shouting something. Sound is always said to carry well over water. This didn't. He'd taken something, or mistaken something. Mary's back was turned, as though on an experience that was over and done with.

When he got back he found Beehernz methodically chewing the cold bacon. 'Sit down, Mr Hopkins. I eat once a day only, usually in the evening. But if it turns out to be midday, so be it.'

And the whisky, what's he done with that? Hopkins realized then what Fraser must have been calling from the boat. He'd taken the bag with the whisky with him, in error, no doubt. The tape recorder was in it, too; Hopkins was left without his standbys, old and new.

'Perhaps you would like to see my potato-bed,' said Beehernz presently. 'I depend on it very extensively. My hens have not laid for nearly a year, although I have not quite lost hope.'

They walked up the gently rising ground to the south, past a washing line from which a long-sleeved vest idly flapped, to an open patch of soil surrounded by a low stone wall. Here Beehernz explained his time-honoured way of cultivating his crop, describing it as a traditional West Highland method. He didn't bury the seed potatoes, but laid them in rows on the surface and dug trenches between the rows, covering them with earth from the trenches as he did so. McGregor had shown him how to do that, or, to be more accurate, McGregor's father.

'Nothing's come up yet,' said Hopkins.

'No, not a green leaf showing.' They stood listening to the gulls crying from every side of them, high up in the deafening blue.

'Why did you try out my piano this morning?' Beehernz asked.

You old wretch, you old monster, how do you know I did?

Back in the living-room, Hopkins brought the piano stool out of the kitchen and drew it up to the table. Then he opened up his document case, moving aside the remnants of the cold food. On this island of Reilig he felt authority leaving him, with no prospect of being replaced by anything else. Authority was scarcely needed in a kingdom of potatoes and seabirds.

I'll begin, he thought, *by calling him by his first name*, then found he had forgotten it. Temporarily of course — he was under stress.

He went on, 'I respect your privacy, and I'm sure you understand that.'

Beehernz replied that he had never considered it at all. 'You need two people to respect privacy, or, indeed, to make it necessary.'

Hopkins took a selection of documents out of his case. Doing this reassured him. The name was Konrad, of course.

'This is our copy of the original contract. You have had your copy signed and returned to you. It didn't at any time specify what your programme was to include. Now, although this wasn't my main object in coming, I've been turning a few thoughts over in my mind, just to see how they strike you.' Beehernz simply repeated the word 'thoughts' with an inappropriate laugh (it was the first time he had laughed). Hopkins continued, 'I take it that you don't, and never did, want to present the monumental Mahler. As I see it, you might begin with some of the early songs — let's say the *Lieder eines fahrenden Gesellen*, the 1884 version, with the piano accompaniment . . .'

Beehernz shook his head slightly with a particularly

sweet smile, which, however, wasn't apologetic, rather it dismissed the whole subject.

'Who was that young woman who was here recently?' he asked.

'You mean Mary Lockett. She was here this morning. So, for that matter, was my assistant Fraser. You told me that you would like them both to leave.'

'I assumed that if they came together, they would prefer to leave together.'

'That was a total misunderstanding. They're no more than acquaintances.'

'A thousand pardons.'

He's not of sound mind – reflected Hopkins. *In that case the contract is void anyway.* He said: 'Am I to understand, then, that you simply don't want to discuss the subject of Mahler?'

Beehernz smiled still. With a show of determination, Hopkins put another set of papers in front of him, and saw him dutifully bend over them.

After twenty minutes, after which he only appeared to be at paragraph two, Beehernz looked up and asked:

'If I die, or even become seriously ill, before conducting this concert, who will be liable to pay this large sum?' He had understood nothing.

'No one would be liable for that,' said Hopkins. It would be *force majeure.*'

Beehernz put both his hands down flat on the papers, as if to eliminate them from his sight. 'Well, I will think about it.'

'Couldn't you decide now?'

'Formerly I could have done so, but now I can only think of one thing at a time.'

Then what are you thinking about now, you old charlatan, you old crook.

'By the way, don't distress yourself about how you are going to get away from the island. McGregor will be back tomorrow. It will be his regular delivery day, when he brings me my few necessities from Iona.'

'What time does he come?'

'He will knock on the door.'

'What time?'

'Early, early, at first light. After that I do not expect him back for another two weeks.'

Hopkins spent the night in the armchair, which, after years of accommodating Beehernz, resolutely refused to fit anyone else. Since there were no bedclothes in the place beyond the plaid, he slept in his shirt and jacket. It was still dark when he suggested putting on the kettle. Beehernz, apparently spry and wakeful, told him that he had never possessed a kettle. 'That may interest you. We never had one, even when I was a child in Leipzig.' He sighed, and went to sleep again. But when the sky grew light, when the unshaven Hopkins had opened the door to McGregor, who said he didn't want tea, thanks, he'd made some in the shed – just as well, Hopkins thought – Beehernz appeared, wearing a tattered *Regenhaut* and a wide-brimmed hat. He was ready not only to go out, but to go away.

'I shall accompany you.'

'You didn't say anything about this last night.'

'I should like to hear that young woman sing again. She cannot have got any further than Iona.'

'You sent her away.'

'I have changed my mind. I should like to hear her sing again. You see, it is so long since I heard music.'

The Prescription

The Prescription

After Petros Zarifi's wife died his shop began to make less and less money. His wife had acted as cashier. That was all over now. The shelves emptied gradually as the unpaid wholesalers refused to supply him with goods. In his tiny room at the back of the shop he had, like many Greek storekeepers, an oleograph in vivid colours of his patron saint, with the motto *Embros* − Forward! But he had now lost all ambition except in the matter of his son Alecco.

The shop was not too badly placed, on the very edge of the Phanar, where Zarifi should have been able to sell to both Greeks and Turks. One of his remaining customers, in fact, was an elderly Stamboullu who worked as dispenser to a prosperous doctor in the Beyazit district. Both old Yousuf and Dr Mehmet drank raki, which they regarded as permissible because it had not been invented in the days of the Prophet. One evening when he was refilling the bottles Zarifi asked Yousuf to speak for him to Mehmet Bey.

'Ask him if he will take my son Alecco, who has just turned fourteen, into his employment.'

'Can't his own relatives provide for him?' asked the old man.

'Don't give a father advice on this matter,' said Zarifi. 'What else does he think about when he lies awake at nights?'

Mehmet Bey took the virtue of compassion seriously. Once he had been told that Zarifi was a *good Greek*, who had won a reputation for honesty, and, possibly as a result, had been unfortunate, he sent word that he would see him.

'Your son can clean my boots and run errands. That is all I have to offer. Don't let him have ambitions. There are too many doctors in Stamboul, and above all, far too many Greeks.'

'Good, well, I understand you, *bey effendi*, you may trust both my son and me.'

It was arranged that Alecco should work and sleep at the doctor's house in Hayreddin Pasha Street. His room was not much larger than a cupboard, but then, neither had it been at home. Loneliness was his trouble, not discomfort. The doctor's wife, Azizié Hanoum, kept to her quarters, and old Yousuf, who was a poor relation of hers, jealously guarded the dispensary, where the drugs must have been arranged on some kind of system since he was able, given time, to make up a prescription when called upon. As to Mehmet Bey himself, his hours were regular. After a sluggish evening visit to the coffee-house to read the newspaper he would return and spend a few hours more than half asleep in the bosom of his family. But Alecco understood very well, or thought he understood, what it was that his father expected him to do.

Polishing the boots of the *hakim bashi* did not take up much of the day. Always obedient, he went about with the doctor as a servant, keeping several paces behind, carrying his bag and his stethoscope. Once a week Mehmet Bey, as a good Moslem, gave his services to the hospital for the poor on the waterfront, and Alecco learned in the wards to recognize the face of leprosy and of death itself. Then, because he was so quick, he began to help a little with the accounts, and from the ledgers he gathered in a few weeks how the practice was run and which were the commonest complaints and how much could be charged for them in each case — always excepting the bills of the very rich, which were presented by Mehmet Bey in person. The doctor, for his part, recognized that this boy was sharp, and did not much like it. A subject race, he reflected, is a penance to the ruler. But he reminded himself that the father was trustworthy and honourable, and in time the son's sharpness might turn into nothing worse than industry, which is harmless.

Every day Alecco asked himself: have I gone one step forward, or one backward? What have I learned that I didn't know yesterday? Books are teachers to those who have none, but the doctor's library reposed behind the wooden shutters of the cupboards fitted into the walls of his consulting-room. His student *Materia Medica* were

there, along with herbals in Arabic and the *Gulistan,* or
Rose Garden of Medicines. Lately he had acquired a brand-
new book, Gray's *Anatomy* in a French translation. Alecco
had seen him turning it over heavily, during the late
afternoon. But it was put away with the others, and there
was no chance to look at it, still less to copy the illus-
trations.

The dispensary, also, was kept locked and bolted. But
that year the month of Ramazan fell in the hot weather,
and both the doctor and old Yousuf, being obliged to fast
all day until sunset, went out through the hours of darkness to take refreshment, Mehmet Bey at the homes of
his friends, Yousuf at the tea-house. Security was less
strict, and the house itself, windowless against the street,
seemed to relax at the end of its tedious day. During the
second week of the fast, Alecco found the door of the
dispensary unfastened.

Just before dawn began to lift, Mehmet Bey returned
and saw that a single candle lamp was burning in his
dispensary. The Greek boy was standing at the bench,
copying out prescriptions. He had also taken down a
measuring-glass, a pestle and a number of bottles and jars.

Bath-boy, *tellak,* son of a whore, the doctor thought.
The hurt pierced deep. His friends had warned him, his
wife had told him he was a fool. But in the end he had
made a burden for his own back.

Alecco was so deeply absorbed that his keen sense of
danger failed him. He did not move until Mehmet Bey
towered close behind him. Then he turned, not dropping

the pen and ink which he had stolen but gripping them closely to him, and stared up with the leaden eyes of a woken sleepwalker at his master.

'I see that you are studying my prescriptions,' said Mehmet Bey. 'I know from experience that you learn quickly.'

He picked up the empty glass. 'Now: make up a medicine for yourself.'

Sweating and trembling, Alecco shook in a measure of this and a measure of that, always keeping his eyes on his master. He could not have said what he was doing. Mehmet Bey, however, saw a dose of aphrodisiac go into the glass, and then the dried flowers of *agnus castus*, which inhibits sex, opium, lavender, *ecballium elaterium*, the most violent of all purgatives, *datura*, either 14 grams, inducing insanity, or 22½ grams (death) and finally mustard and cinnamon. Silently he pointed to the fuller's earth, which prevents the patient from vomiting. Alecco added a handful.

'Drink!'

The doctor's voice, raised to a pitch of sacred rage, woke up Azizié Hanoum, and standing terrified in her old wrapper at the door of the women's quarters she saw her husband seize the Greek boy by the nose, from which water poured out, and force his head backwards to dislocation point while something black as pitch ran from the measuring-glass down his throat.

*   *   *

In the morning Alecco, who had been crammed into his room unconscious, appeared smiling with the doctor's cleaned boots in his hands. Mehmet Bey made a sign to avert evil.

'You're well? You're alive?'

'My prescription did me a world of good.'

The doctor called his servants and had him turned out of the house. Picking himself up, Alecco walked away with fourteen-year-old jauntiness along the new horse tramway until he was out of sight. Not until he reached the foot of the Galata Bridge did his will-power give way and he collapsed groaning like vermin on a dung-hill.

Preparing slowly for his rounds, Mehmet Bey at first congratulated himself, since if the boy had died he was not quite certain how he would have stood with the law. But the household's peace was destroyed. Old Yousuf was so perturbed by the mess in the dispensary that he collapsed with a slight stroke. He had never been able to read, and now that the drugs were out of order he could find nothing. Azizié Hanoum poured reproaches on her husband and declared that if the little Greek had been better treated he could have been trained to help Yousuf. Zarifi mourned his son, who did not return either to the Phanar or to Hayreddin Pasha Street. In a few months the grocer's shop was bankrupt.

Alecco had been picked up on the waterfront by a Greek ship's cook, coming back on board after a night's absence. He had some confused idea of conciliating the captain, who, he knew, was short of a boy. The *Andromeda* was an irregular trading vessel carrying mail via Malta and Gibraltar, and by the time she reached London Alecco had been seasick to such an extent that he was clear of the poison's last traces. This seemed a kind of providence; he could never have cheated Death without some help. The captain had fancied him from the start, and when the crew were paid off at Albert Docks he gave him five pounds in English money to make a good start in life.

Ten years later Dr Mehmet's career had reached its highest point and was also (he was sixty-five) approaching its end. Having been called, not for the first time, for consultation at the Old Serail, he settled down for a long waiting period before an attendant arrived to escort him to the ante-rooms. He took a seat overlooking the Sea of Marmara, and resigned himself. In contemplation of the lazing water, he allowed his energies to sleep. The ladies here were the old and the pensioned-off, but the appointment was an honour.

Quite without warning, and faintly disagreeable, was the appearance of a secretary: Lelia Hanoum had wished for a second opinion, and he had the honour to present a distinguished young colleague who had hurried here from another appointment. But when a young man walked in wearing a black *stambouline*, the professional's frock-coat, and followed by a servant carrying his bag and stethoscope, Mehmet Bey knew not only who he was, but that he had been expecting him.

'I decline to accept you as a colleague, Alexander Zarifi.'

'I am qualified,' Dr Zarifi replied.

'Your word is not good enough.'

Alecco took out from the upper pocket of his *stambouline* a card printed in gilt, which showed that he had recently been appointed to attend the Serail. This could not be contradicted, and after putting it away he said:

'I am honoured, then, to join you as a consultant.' He waited for the usual, in fact necessary, reply: 'The honour is mine,' but instead Mehmet Bey said loudly: 'There is no need for us to waste time in each other's company. I know the case history of Lelia Hanoum, you may consult my notes. I have already made the diagnosis. Last year the patient complained of acute pain in the left side and a distention as though a ball or globe was rising from the abdomen to the throat. Palpitations, fits of crying, quantities of wind passed per rectum. A typical case of hysteria, all too common in the Serail, and entirely the result of an ill-balanced regimen. I advised firm treatment, iron pills and a gentian tonic. Recently, however, she has described the initial pain as on the right side. Accordingly I have changed my diagnosis to acute appendicitis, and I propose to operate as soon as permission can be got from the Palace. She is rather old for the operation to be success-ful, but that is in God's hands.'

'I cannot agree,' Dr Zarifi replied. 'The very fact that the patient is uncertain whether she feels pain on the left or the right side means that we must look beneath her symptoms for an unconscious or subconscious factor. During my training in Vienna I was fortunate enough to work with Dr Josef Breuer, the great specialist in hysteria.

It is for the woman herself to lead us to the hidden factor, perhaps under hypnosis. It is my belief that there is no need for medication, still less surgical interference. We must aim at setting her free.'

'Well, now I have your opinion,' said Mehmet Bey. 'If I reject it, it is because I have studied the art of healing, not so much from personal ambition as to answer the simplest of all appeals – *hastayim*, I am ill. I accept that since we last met you have had the advantage of a good training, but your nature will not have changed. You are still Alexander Zarifi. What is more, there are universal laws, which govern all human beings, not excepting men of science. Cast your memory back, and answer me this question: Knowledge is good, but what is the use of knowledge without honesty?'

Dr Alecco looked down at the ground, and withdrew his diagnosis.

At Hiruharama

At Hiruharama

Mr Tanner was anxious to explain how it was that he had a lawyer in the family, so that when they all decided to sell up and quit New Zealand there had been someone they could absolutely trust with the legal business.

That meant that he had to say something about his grandfather, who had been an orphan from Stamford in Lincolnshire and was sent out to a well-to-do family north of Auckland, supposedly as an apprentice, but it turned out that he was to be more or less of a servant. He cleaned the knives, saw to the horses, waited at table and chopped the wood. On an errand to a dry goods store in Auckland he met Kitty, Mr Tanner's grandmother. She had come out from England as a governess, and she too found she was really wanted as a servant. She was sixteen, and Tanner asked her to wait for three years while he saved his wages, and then to marry him. All this was at a Methodist social, say a couple of weeks later. 'What family have you got back home?' Kitty asked him. Tanner replied just the one sister. Younger or older? Older. She probably thinks I'm a skilled craftsman by now. She probably reckons I'm made. – Haven't you sent word to her lately? – Not lately. – Best write to her now, anyway, said Kitty, and tell her how it is between us. I should be glad to have a new relation, I haven't many. – I'll think it over, he said. Kitty realized then that he could neither read nor write.

They had to start in a remote country place. The land round Auckland at that time was ten shillings an acre, a third of the price going to build the new churches and schools, but where Tanner and Kitty went, north of Awanui, there weren't any churches and schools, and it was considerably cheaper. They didn't have to buy their place, it had been left deserted, and yet it had something you could give a thousand pounds for and not get, and that was a standpipe giving constant clear water from an underground well. But whoever lived there had given up, because of the loneliness and because it was such poor country. Don't picture a shack, though. There were two rooms, one with a stove and one with a bedstead, and a third one at the back for a vegetable store. Tanner grew root vegetables and went into Awanui twice a week with the horse and dray. Kitty stayed behind, because they'd taken on two hundred chickens and a good few pigs.

Tanner turned over in his mind what he'd say to his wife when she told him she was going to have a child. When she did tell him, which wasn't for another two years or so, by the way, he didn't hear her at first, because a northerly was blowing and neither of them could expect to hear each other. When he did catch what she was saying, he hitched up and drove into Awanui. The doctor was at his midday dinner, which he took at a boarding-house higher up the main street. When he got back and into his consulting-room Tanner asked him what were the life statistics of the North Island.

'Do you mean the death statistics?' the doctor asked.

'They'll do just as well,' said Tanner.

'No one dies here except from drink or drowning. Out of three thousand people in Taranaki Province there hasn't been a single funeral in the last sixteen months and only twenty-four sick and infirm. You may look upon me as a poor man.'

'What about women in childbirth?' asked Tanner.

The doctor didn't have any figures for women dying in childbirth, but he looked sharply at Tanner and asked him when his child was due.

'You don't know, of course. Well, don't ask me if it's going to be twins. Nature didn't intend us to know that.' He began to write in his notebook. 'Where are you living?'

'It's off the road to Houhora, you turn off to the right after twelve miles.'

'What's it called?'

'Hiruharama.'

'Don't know it. That's not a Maori name.'

'I think it means Jerusalem,' said Tanner.

'Are there any other women about the place?'

'No.'

'I mean someone who could come in and look after things while your wife's laid up. Who's your nearest neighbour?' Tanner told him there was no one except a man called Brinkman, who came over sometimes. He was about nine or ten miles off at Stony Loaf.

'And he has a wife?'

'No, he hasn't, that's what he complains about. You couldn't ask a woman to live out there.'

'You can ask a woman to live anywhere,' said the doctor. 'He's a crank, I dare say.'

'He's a dreamer,' Tanner replied. 'I should term Brinkman a dreamer.'

'I was thinking in terms of washing the sheets, that sort of thing. If there's no one else, can you manage about the house yourself for a few days?'

'I can do anything about the house,' said Tanner.

'You don't drink?'

Tanner shook his head, wondering if the doctor did. He asked if he shouldn't bring his wife with him for a consultation next time he drove over to Awanui. The doctor looked out of his window at the bone-shaking old dray with its iron-rimmed wheels. 'Don't.'

He tore the prescription out of his notebook. 'Get this for your wife. It's calcium water. When you want me to come, you'll have to send for me. But don't let that worry you. Often by the time I arrive I'm not needed.'

Other patients had arrived and were sitting on the wooden benches on the verandah. Some had empty medicine bottles for a refill. There was a man with his right arm strapped up, several kids with their mothers, and a woman who looked well enough but seemed to be in tears for some reason or other. — Well, you see life in the townships.

Tanner went over to the post office, where there was free pen and ink if you wanted it, and wrote a letter to his sister. — But wait a minute, surely he couldn't read or write? Evidently by that time he could. Mr Tanner's guess was that although Kitty was a quiet girl, very quiet, she'd refused to marry him until he'd got the hang of it. — Tanner wrote: My darling old sister. Well, it's come to pass and either a girl or a boy will be added unto us. It would be a help if you could send us a book on the subject. We have now a hundred full-grown hens and a further hundred at point of lay, and a good stand of potatoes. — After mailing the letter he bought soap, thread, needles, canned fish, tea and sugar. When he drove out of Awanui he stopped at the last homestead, where he knew a man called Parrish who kept racing-pigeons. Some of them, in fact, were just arriving back at their loft. Parrish had cut the entrances to the nests down very small, and every time a bird got home it had to squeeze past a bell on a string so that the tinkling sound gave warning. They were all Blue Chequers, the only kind, Parrish declared, that a sane man would want to keep. Tanner explained his predicament and asked for the loan of two birds. Parrish didn't mind, because Hiruharama, Tanner's place, was on a more or less direct line from

Awanui to Te Paki station, and that was the line his pigeons flew.

'If you'd have lived over the other way I couldn't have helped you,' Parrish said.

A Maori boy took the young birds out as soon as they were four months old and tossed them at three miles, ten miles, twenty miles, always in the same direction, north-north-west of Awanui.

'As long as they can do fifteen miles,' said Tanner.

'They can do two hundred and fifty.'

'How long will it take them to do fifteen miles?'

'Twenty minutes in clear weather,' said Parrish.

The Maori boy chose out two birds and packed them into a wicker hamper, which Tanner wedged into the driver's seat of the dray.

'Have you got them numbered in some way?' Tanner asked.

'I don't need to. I know them all,' said Parrish.

He added that they would need rock salt, so Tanner drove back into the town once more to buy the rock salt and a sack of millet. By the time he got to Hiruharama the dark clear night sky was pressing in on every side. I ought to have taken you with me, he told Kitty. She said she had been all right. He hadn't, though, he'd been worried. You mean you've forgotten something at the stores, said Kitty. Tanner went out to the dray and fetched the pigeons, still shifting about and conferring quietly in their wicker basket.

'Here's one thing more than you asked for,' he said. They found room for them in the loft above the vegetable store. The Blue Chequers were the prettiest things about the place.

The sister in England did send a book, although it didn't arrive for almost a year. In any case, it only had one chapter of a practical nature. Otherwise, it was religious in tone. But meanwhile Kitty's calculations couldn't have been far out, because more or less when they expected it the pains came on strong enough for Tanner to send for the doctor.

He had made the pigeons' nests out of packing-cases. They ought to have flown out daily for exercise, but he hadn't been able to manage that. Still, they looked fair enough, a bit dishevelled, but not so that you'd notice. It was four o'clock, breezy, but not windy. He took them out into the bright air which, even that far from the coast, was full of the salt of the ocean. How to toss a pigeon he had no idea. He opened the basket, and before he could think what to do next they were out and up into the blue. He watched in terror as after reaching a certain height they began turning round in tight circles as though puzzled or lost. Then, apparently sighting something on the horizon that they knew, they set off strongly towards Awanui. – Say twenty minutes for them to get to Parrish's loft. Ten minutes for Parrish or the Maori boy to walk up the street to the doctor's. Two and a half hours for the doctor to drive over, even allowing for his losing the way once. Thirty seconds for him to get down from his trap and open his bag. –

At five o'clock Tanner went out to see to the pigs and

hens. At six Kitty was no better and no worse. She lay
there quietly, sweating from head to foot. 'I can hear
someone coming,' she said, not from Awanui, though, it
was along the top road. Tanner thought it must be Brinkman. 'Why, yes, it must be six months since he came,'
said Kitty, as though she was making conversation. Who
else, after all, could it have been on the top road? The
track up there had a deep rounded gutter each side which
made it awkward to drive along. They could hear the
screeching and rattling of his old buggy, two wheels in
the gutter, two out. 'He's stopped at the gully now to let
his horse drink,' said Kitty. 'He'll have to let it walk the
rest of the way.' – 'He'll have to turn round when he
gets here and start right back,' said Tanner.

There used to be a photograph of Brinkman somewhere, but Mr Tanner didn't know what had become of
it, and he believed it hadn't been a good likeness in any
case. – Of course, in the circumstances, as he'd come
eight miles over a rough road, he had to be asked to put
up his horse for a while, and come in.

Like most people who live on their own Brinkman
continued with the course of his thoughts, which were
more real to him than the outside world's commotion.
Walking straight into the front room he stopped in front
of the piece of mirror-glass tacked over the sink and
looked fixedly into it.

'I'll tell you something, Tanner, I thought I caught
sight of my first grey hairs this morning.'

'I'm sorry to hear that.'

Brinkman looked round. 'I see the table isn't set.'

'I don't want you to feel that you're not welcome,' said Tanner, 'but Kitty's not well. She told me to be sure that you came in and rested a while, but she's not well. Truth is, she's in labour.'

'Then she won't be cooking dinner this evening, then?'

'You mean you were counting on having it here?'

'My half-yearly dinner with you and Mrs Tanner, yis, that's about it.'

'What day is it, then?' asked Tanner, somewhat at random. It was almost too much for him at that moment to realize that Brinkman existed. He seemed like a stranger, perhaps from a foreign country, not understanding how ordinary things were done or said.

Brinkman made no attempt to leave, but said, 'Last time I came here we started with canned toheroas. Your wife set them in front of me. I'm not sure that they had an entirely good effect on the intestines. Then we had fried eggs and excellent jellied beetroot, a choice between tea or Bovo, bread and butter and unlimited quantities of treacle. I have a note of all this in my daily journal. That's not to say, however, that I came over here simply to take dinner with you. It wasn't for the drive, either, although I'm always glad to have the opportunity of a change of scene and to read a little in Nature's book. No, I've come today, as I came formerly, for the sake of hearing a woman's voice.'

Had Tanner noticed, he went on, that there were no native songbirds in the territory? At that moment there was a crying, or a calling, from the next room such as Tanner had never heard before, not in a shipwreck — and he had been in a wreck — not in a slaughterhouse.

'Don't put yourself out on my account,' said Brinkman. 'I'm going to sit here until you come back and have a quiet smoko.'

The doctor drove up bringing with him his wife's widowed sister, who lived with them and was a nurse, or had been a nurse. Tanner came out of the bedroom covered with blood, something like a butcher. He told the doctor he'd managed to deliver the child, a girl, in fact he'd wrapped it in a towel and tucked it up in the washbasket. The doctor took him back into the bedroom and made him sit down. The nurse put down the things she'd brought with her and looked round for the tea-tin. Brinkman sat there, as solid as his chair. 'You may be wondering who I am,' he said. 'I'm a neighbour, come over for dinner. I think of myself as one of the perpetually welcome.' 'Suit yourself,' said the sister-in-law. The doctor emerged, moving rather faster than he usually did. 'Please to go in there and wash the patient. I'm going to take a look at the afterbirth. The father put it out with the waste.'

There Tanner had made his one oversight. It wasn't the afterbirth, it was a second daughter, smaller, but a twin. — But how come, if both of them were girls, that Mr Tanner himself still had the name of Tanner? Well, the Tanners went on to have nine more children, some of them boys, and one of those boys was Mr Tanner's father. That evening, when the doctor came in from the yard with the messy scrap, he squeezed it as though he was wringing it out to dry, and it opened its mouth and the colder air of the kitchen rushed in and she'd got her start in life. After that the Tanners always had one of those tinplate mottoes hung up on the wall – Throw Nothing Away. You could get them then at the hardware store. – And this was the point that Mr Tanner had been wanting to make all along – whereas the first daughter never got to be anything in particular, this second little girl grew up to be a lawyer with a firm in Wellington, and she did very well.

All the time Brinkman continued to sit there by the table and smoke his pipe. Two more women born into the world! It must have seemed to him that if this sort of thing went on there should be a good chance, in the end, for him to acquire one for himself. Meanwhile, they would have to serve dinner sometime.

Not Shown

Not Shown

Lady P lived at Tailfirst, which was not shown to the public. Fothergill was the resident administrator, or dogsbody, at Tailfirst Farm, which was shown 1 April to end October, Mon., Wed., Sat.: no coach-parties, no backpackers, guide dogs by arrangement, WC, small shop. It was the old Home Farm, sympathetically rebuilt in red brick between 1892 and 1894 by Philip Webb (a good example of his later manner), the small herb and lavender garden possibly suggested by Gertrude Jekyll. The National Trust had steadfastly refused to take it over; still, they can make mistakes, like the rest of us.

'Now Fothergill, as to the room stewards,' said Lady P., returning with frighteningly renewed energies from the Maldives.

'The ladies . . .'

'The Trust calls them room stewards . . .'

'Two of them, of course, are your own recommendations – Mrs Feare, who was at the Old Pottery Shop until it closed, and Mrs Twine, who was dinner lady at the village school.'

'Until *that* closed. Faithful souls both.'

'I'm sure they are, and that is my great difficulty.'

'Don't confuse yourself with detail. You must treasure Twine and Feare, and dispense with Mrs Horrabin.'

'I should very much like to do that,' said Fothergill.

Lady P. looked at him sharply. 'I'm told in the village that you only engaged her last Wednesday. Now, in any group of employees, and perhaps particularly with low-paid employees, a dominating figure creates discord.'

'Do you know Mrs Horrabin well, Lady P?' asked Fothergill.

'Of course not. I've been obliged to meet her, I think twice, on my Recreation Committee. She comes from the Industrial Estate at Battisford, as you ought to know.'

'I do know it.'

'You don't look well, you know, Fothergill. When you came into the room I thought, the man doesn't look well. Are you still worrying about anything?'

He collected himself for a moment. 'In what way am I to get rid of Mrs Horrabin?'

'I'm sure you don't want me to tell you how to do your job,' said Lady P.

'I do want you to tell me.'

Fothergill lived in one of the attics (not shown) at the Farm, on a salary so small that it was difficult to see how he had survived for the past year. Undoubtedly there was something not quite right about him, or by the time he was fifty-six — if that was his real age — he would be married (perhaps he had been), and he would certainly by now have found some better employment. Lady P, who found it better in every way not to leave such things to her husband, had drafted the advertisement which was specifically aimed at applicants with something not quite right about them, who would come cheap: 'Rent-free accommodation, remote, peaceful situation, ample free time, suit writer.' Fothergill wasn't a writer, but then he soon discovered there wasn't much free time either.

'I do want you to tell me,' he repeated.

He had known very little about architecture when he came, nothing about tile hanging, weather boarding, lead box-guttering or late Victorian electrical fittings, and he had never heard of Philip Webb. He learned these things between maintaining the garden, the very old Land Rover and the still older petrol mower. But the home-made damson cordial was manufactured and supplied by a Pakistani-owned firm in Sheffield, no trouble there, and to his surprise, Mrs Feare and Mrs Twine had agreed to come. 'You're a novelty for them,' said the man who came to clean out the cess-pit. It was gratifying to Fothergill to be described as a novelty.

So far there had been worryingly few visitors, but he disposed carefully of his small force. Mrs Twine couldn't stand for too long, and was best off in the dining-room where there was a solid table to lean against; on the other hand, she was sharper than Mrs Feare, who let people linger in the conservatory and nick the tomatoes.

Mrs Feare was more at home in the shop with the fudge and postcards, and her ten-year-old son biked up after school to work out the day's VAT on his calculator. Mrs Twine also fancied herself in the shop, but had no son to offer. Fothergill hurried about between the garden, the white-painted drawing-room and the cash-desk. Each day solved itself, by closing time, without complaints. A remote, peaceful situation.

Mrs Horrabin had driven up to the front door of the Farm at 9 a.m. last Tuesday. To avoid shouting out of the bedroom window he had come downstairs, unbarred, unlocked and unopened. 'The house is not shown today, madam. Can I help you at all?'

'We'll see,' said Mrs Horrabin.

Hugely, beigely, she got out of her Sunny, and with a broad white smile told him her name.

'I've decided to take over here.'

'I'm afraid there are no vacancies.'

'Shirley Twine won't be coming back after the end of this week.'

'She said nothing . . .'

'She'll take a hint.'

'Mrs Feare . . .'

'I'll give her a hint as well. They won't either of them break their hearts over it, they can get another little job easily enough.' She stared at him boldly and unpeaceably. 'Some can, some can't.'

Although from long habit Fothergill pretended not to understand her, he was in no way surprised. He was pretty sure he had never met Mrs Horrabin before, but that didn't mean that through one of life's thousand unhappy coincidences she might not know something unacceptable about him. He had lived in so many places, and so often left them in a hurry.

'Didn't you once work as a credit manager in Basingstoke?' she asked now. 'An uncle of mine lives there.'

She belonged to the tribe of torturers. Why pretend they don't exist?

'You have it in mind,' he said, 'to take away my last chance.'

Mrs Horrabin ignored this. 'I know what's wrong with this place. You've got these two old boilers standing in the corners of the rooms and they make people afraid to come in at all. In any case they don't particularly want to look at what's on show, they want to have a good poke around. They want to see the bedrooms and the john.'

In default of a decent piece of rope Fothergill had placed a handwritten card, PRIVATE, on the front stairs. Mrs Horrabin actually trod on it — visitors wearing stiletto heels not admitted — on her way up. In rage and disgust he followed her into the never-used, pomegranate-papered front bedroom where, marching in, she dragged down the blinds.

'It isn't necessary to restrict the light in here,' he said, clinging to his professional status, 'there are no water-colours.'

'I like them down. Just for half an hour or so.'

She sat down on the double bed, whose box-springs reverberated, and took off her jacket. She was wearing a very low-necked blouse, with machine embroidery. 'I don't believe you know what to do next,' she said.

Fothergill cried, 'It's only twenty past nine in the morning.' It was not quite what he had meant to say. He went on, 'You're making a grotesque mistake.'

'Well, perhaps I am, we'll have to see,' said Mrs Horrabin. 'At least, though, you've got your own teeth. You can't go wrong about that, you can always catch the gleam of dentures. Anyway, the choice isn't so wide round here.'

But from her great beige bag, which she had never so far left hold of, a great monotonous chirp began, like a demented pipit.

'That'll be Mr Horrabin outside in your drive.' She opened her bag and took out her mobile phone. 'Tweety calling Bub . . .'

'Your husband knows you're here?'

'He always knows where I am. He isn't against my enjoying myself, he stretches a point there, but he likes to feel included.'

'Included in what way?'

'He's an area salesman for alternative medicines . . . He wants me at home, it seems, so I'm letting you off for this morning . . . But I'll be back tomorrow. We'll be able to manage quite well between us.'

He shouted, 'You have robbed me of Mrs Feare and Mrs Twine, you have taken away my peace of mind, and what's worse I find you completely unattractive.' Or perhaps he had never said the words aloud, since Mrs Horrabin was standing self-approvingly in front of the cheval glass, with the calm smile of the powerful, smoothing the shoulders of her jacket.

While Fothergill allowed himself to think backwards into the trap of his mind, Lady P. had been talking on, passing to many other topics, and now gracefully returned. He mustn't blame himself too much, she said, for the disappointing figures. Apart from the fact that they didn't do teas, the great drawback was that nothing interesting had ever happened at Tailfirst Farm. Not a murder, she didn't mean that, although it would certainly create some interest, but perhaps some sad and unexpected accident . . . She laughed a little, to show that a joke had been intended, but saw that Fothergill had been quite prepared to agree with her. He hasn't much spirit, she thought. Probably he never thinks about anything except keeping his job.

Desideratus

Desideratus

Jack Digby's mother never gave him anything. Perhaps, as a poor woman, she had nothing to give, or perhaps she was not sure how to divide anything between the nine children. His godmother, Mrs Piercy, the poulterer's wife, did give him something, a keepsake, in the form of a gilt medal. The date on it was September the 12th, 1663, which happened to be Jack's birthday, although by the time she gave it him he was eleven years old. On the back there was the figure of an angel and a motto, *Desideratus*, which, perhaps didn't fit the case too well, since Mrs Digby could have done with fewer, rather than more, children. However, it had taken the godmother's fancy.

Jack thanked her, and she advised him to stow it away safely, out of reach of the other children. Jack was amazed that she should think anywhere was out of the reach of his little sisters. 'You should have had it earlier, when you were born,' said Mrs Piercy, 'but those were hard times.' Jack told her that he was very glad to have something of which he could say, This is my own, and she answered, though not with much conviction, that he mustn't set too much importance on earthly possessions.

He kept the medal with him always, only transferring it, as the year went by, from his summer to his winter breeches. But anything you carry about with you in your pocket you are bound to lose sooner or later. Jack had an errand to do in Hending, but there was nothing on the road that day, neither horse nor cart, no hope of cadging a lift, so after waiting for an hour or so he began to walk over by the hill path.

After about a mile the hill slopes away sharply towards Watching, which is not a village and never was, only a single great house standing among its outbuildings almost at the bottom of the valley. Jack stopped there for a while to look down at the smoke from the chimneys and to calculate, as anyone might have done, the number of dinners that were being cooked there that day.

If he dropped or lost his keepsake he did not know it at the time, for as is commonly the case he didn't miss it until he got home again. Then he went through his pockets, but the shining medal was gone and he could only repeat, 'I had it when I started out.' His brothers and sisters were of no help at all. They had seen nothing. What brother or sister likes being asked such questions?

The winter frosts began and at Michaelmas Jack had the day off school and thought, I had better try going that way again. He halted, as before, at the highest point, to look down at the great house and its chimneys, and then at the ice under his feet, for all the brooks, ponds, and runnels were frozen on every side of him, all hard as bone. In a little hole or depression just to the left hand of the path, something no bigger than a small puddle, but deep, and by now set thick with greenish ice as clear as glass, he saw, through the transparency of the ice, at the depth of perhaps twelve inches, the keepsake that Mrs Piercy had given him.

He had nothing in his hand to break the ice. Well then, Jack Digby, jump on it, but that got him nowhere, seeing that his wretched pair of boots was soaked right through. 'I'll wait until the ice has gone,' he thought. 'The season is turning, we'll get a thaw in a day or two.'

On the next Sunday, by which time the thaw had set in, he was up there again, and made straight for the little hole or declivity, and found nothing. It was empty, after that short time, of ice and even of water. And because the idea of recovering the keepsake had occupied his whole mind that day, the disappointment made him feel lost, like a stranger to the country. Then he noticed that there was an earthenware pipe laid straight down the side of the hill, by way of a drain, and that this must very likely have carried off the water from his hole, and everything in it. No mystery as to where it led, it joined another pipe with a wider bore, and so down, I suppose, to the stable-yards, thought Jack. His Desideratus had been washed down there, he was as sure of that now as if he'd seen it go.

Jack had never been anywhere near the house before, and did not care to knock at the great kitchen doors for

fear of being taken for a beggar. The yards were empty.
Either the horses had been taken out to work now that
the ground was softer or else – which was hard to believe
– there were no horses at Watching. He went back to the
kitchen wing and tried knocking at a smallish side entrance. A man came out dressed in a black gown, and
stood there peering and trembling.

'Why don't you take off your cap to me?' he asked.

Jack took it off, and held it behind his back, as though
it belonged to someone else.

'That is better. Who do you think I am?'

'No offence, sir,' Jack replied, 'but you look like an old
schoolmaster.'

'I am a schoolmaster, that is, I am tutor to this great
house. If you have a question to ask, you may ask it of
me.'

With one foot still on the step, Jack related the story
of his godmother's keepsake.

'Very good,' said the tutor, 'you have told me enough.
Now I am going to test your memory. You will agree
that this is not only necessary, but just.'

'I can't see that it has anything to do with my matter,'
said Jack.

'Oh, but you tell me that you dropped this-or-that in
such-and-such a place, and in that way lost what had
been given to you. How can I tell that you have truthfully
remembered all this? You know that when I came to the
door you did not remember to take your cap off.'

'But that –'

'You mean that was only lack of decent manners, and shows that you come from a family without self-respect. Now, let us test your memory. Do you know the Scriptures?'

Jack said that he did, and the tutor asked him what happened, in the fourth chapter of the Book of Job, to Eliphaz the Temanite, when a vision came to him in the depth of the night.

'A spirit passed before his face, sir, and the hair of his flesh stood up.'

'The hair of his flesh stood up,' the tutor repeated. 'And now, have they taught you any Latin?' Jack said that he knew the word that had been on his medal, and that it was *Desideratus*, meaning long wished-for.

'That is not an exact translation,' said the tutor. Jack thought, he talks for talking's sake.

'Have you many to teach, sir, in this house?' he asked, but the tutor half closed his eyes and said, 'None, none at all. God has not blessed Mr Jonas or either of his late wives with children. Mr Jonas has not multiplied.'

If that is so, Jack thought, this schoolmaster can't have much work to do. But now at last here was somebody with more sense, a house-keeperish-looking woman, come to see why the side-door was open and letting cold air into the passages. 'What does the boy want?' she asked.

'He says he is in search of something that belongs to him.'

'You might have told him to come in, then, and given him a glass of wine in the kitchen,' she said, less out of kindness than to put the tutor in his place. 'He would have been glad of that, I daresay.'

Jack told her at once that at home they never touched wine. 'That's a pity,' said the housekeeper. 'Children who are too strictly prohibited generally turn out drunkards.' There's no pleasing these people, Jack thought.

His whole story had to be gone through again, and then again when they got among the servants in one of the pantries. Yet really there was almost nothing to tell, the only remarkable point being that he should have seen the keepsake clearly through almost a foot of ice. Still nothing was said as to its being found in any of the yards or ponds.

Among all the to-ing and fro-ing another servant came in, the man who attended on the master, Mr Jonas, himself. His arrival caused a kind of disquiet, as though he were a foreigner. The master, he said, had got word that there was a farm-boy, or a schoolboy, in the kitchens, come for something that he thought was his property.

'But all this is not for Mr Jonas's notice,' cried the tutor. 'It's a story of child's stuff, a child's mischance, not at all fitting for him to look into.'

The man repeated that the master wanted to see the boy.

The other part of the house, the greater part, where Mr Jonas lived, was much quieter, the abode of gentry. In the main hall Mr Jonas himself stood with his back to the fire. Jack had never before been alone or dreamed of being alone with such a person. What a pickle, he thought, my godmother, Mrs Piercy, has brought me into.

'I daresay you would rather have a sum of money,' said Mr Jonas, not loudly, 'than whatever it is that you have lost.'

Jack was seized by a painful doubt. To be honest, if it was to be a large sum of money, he would rather have that than anything. But Mr Jonas went on, 'However, you had better understand me more precisely. Come with me.' And he led the way, without even looking round to see that he was followed.

At the foot of the wide staircase Jack called out from behind, 'I think, sir, I won't go any further. What I lost can't be here.'

'It's poor-spirited to say "I won't go any further",' said Mr Jonas.

Was it possible that on these dark upper floors no one else was living, no one was sleeping? They were like a sepulchre, or a barn at the end of winter. Through the tall passages, over uneven floors, Mr Jonas, walking ahead, carried a candle in its candlestick in each hand, the flames pointing straight upwards. I am very far from home, thought Jack. Then, padding along behind the master of the house, and still twisting his cap in one hand, he saw in dismay that the candle flames were blown over to the left, and a door was open to the right.

'Am I to go in there with you, sir?'

'Are you afraid to go into a room?'

Inside it was dark and in fact the room probably never got much light, the window was so high up. There was a glazed jug and basin, which reflected the candles, and a large bed which had no curtains, or perhaps, in spite of the cold, they had been drawn back. There seemed to be neither quilts nor bedding, but a boy was lying there in a linen gown, with his back towards Jack, who saw that he had red or reddish hair, much the same colour as his own.

'You may go near him, and see him more clearly,' Mr Jonas said. 'His arm is hanging down, what do you make of that?'

'I think it hangs oddly, sir.'

He remembered what the tutor had told him, that Mr Jonas had not multiplied his kind, and asked, 'What is his name, sir?' To this he got no answer.

Mr Jonas gestured to him to move nearer, and said, 'You may take his hand.'

'No, sir, I can't do that.'

'Why not? You must touch other children very often. Wherever you live, you must sleep the Lord knows how many in a bed.'

'Only three in a bed at ours,' Jack muttered.

'Then touch, touch.'

'No, sir, no, I can't touch the skin of him!'

Mr Jonas set down his candles, went to the bed, took the boy's wrist and turned it, so that the fingers opened. From the open fingers he took Jack's medal, and gave it back to him.

'Was it warm or cold?' they asked him later. Jack told them that it was cold. Cold as ice? Perhaps not quite as cold as that.

'You have what you came for,' said Mr Jonas. 'You have taken back what was yours. Note that I don't deny it was yours.'

He did not move again, but stood looking down at the whiteish heap on the bed. Jack was more afraid of staying than going, although he had no idea how to find his way through the house, and was lucky to come upon a back staircase which ended not where he had come in but among the sculleries, where he managed to draw back the double bolts and get out into the fresh air.

'Did the boy move,' they asked him, 'when the medal was taken away from him?' But by this time Jack was making up the answers as he went along. He preferred, on the whole, not to think much about Watching. It struck him, though, that he had been through a good deal to get back his godmother's present, and he quite often wondered how much money Mr Jonas would in fact have offered him, if he had had the sense to accept it. Anyone who has ever been poor – even if not as poor as Jack Digby – will sympathize with him in this matter.